TENDERNESS AND OTHER STOR
of five long-form short sto
e-books by Island Shorts. It ..
well as e-book format.

Technology closes spaces and opens worlds. In the publishing industry, the advent of e-books allows people living almost anywhere on the planet to download a story instantaneously. And it makes way for small publishers to come together to put their art into the world with relative ease. In Minden Hills, those new digital pathways are already being trodden by author and playwright Michael Fay.

~ *review by Jenn Watt, The Minden Times*

It all started with a small ad in the community newsletter: Writing Lessons, contact Michael Fay, and that is why eight of us were gathered around a large wooden table. We were there to learn W.O. Mitchell's Freefall method, as modified by Michael. Put your pen to paper and write, he told us, don't worry about grammar, sentence structure or paragraphing – just write. And so we did, memories poured forth, the smell of freshly washed laundry, the sound of a train whistle on a cold winter night. For six days we wrote and on the seventh we rested, while Michael studied very single word we had written and picked out the best phrase, sentence or paragraph that he read back in class. With Michael's gentle encouragement, we gained confidence, reality turned into fiction, short stories emerged, and we were on our way to becoming writers.

~*Shirley Black, Calgary*

Tenderness
and other stories

by

J. Michael Fay

9·12·19

For Katie
From Michael

IslandCatEditions

Minden, Bequia

Copyright © 2019, J. Michael Fay

All rights reserved. The use of any part of this publication reproduced, transmitted in any form or by any means, electronic, mechanical, photocopying, recording, or otherwise, or stored in a retrieval systems, without the prior written consent of the publisher – or in the case of photocopying or other reprographic copying, a licence from Access Copyright – is an infringement of copyright law.

Published worldwide by
IslandCatEditions
ISBN print: 978-1-927950-15-9
ISBN mobi: 978-1-927950-16-6
ISBN ePub: 978-1-927950-17-3

Original Cover Painting and all interior artwork: Karen Sloan
Cover and Interior Design and Listing: Human Powered Design

IslandCatEditions
susanmtoy@gmail.com

For Fay, as always

Contents

The Whirlabout 1

The Healer 27

Passion 61

Draft Dodger? 89

Tenderness 129

Introduction

As Michael says very often these days, we've been together for 43 years and we have a very good life in these northern woods. This is where these stories were written: our sun-dappled house on a hill overlooking a lake in Minden, Ontario.

They were conceived in even more northerly woods in the summer of 1976. That summer Michael studied at the Banff School of the Arts under the tutelage of the crème de la crème of Canadian writers using the freefall method championed by W. O Mitchell. Some of the material became stories published in magazines, and a version of The Healer was published as a text for adult literacy students. The stories in this book sprang from typewritten pages that yellowed for years in a banker's box we shuffled through multiple moves and reorganizations. They languished primarily because the length they needed to get to the end from the beginning, unfolding according to their natural need, did not fit the publishing conventions of the time: too long for short stories, too short for novellas. But ePublishing threw out those conventions. So, in 2014 Michael pulled out that banker's box and returned to writing fiction. He calls these stories long-form short stories.

They reflect pivotal incidents in Michael's life. A life impacted by conflict: the Vietnam War he immigrated to Canada so as not to fight; the sometimes subtle social battles of both his professional and his personal life; and historical conflicts he loved to research and deeply imagine.

Michael grew up in a stolid Catholic community in Cincinnati, Ohio, where the world was simply divided between people of Italian (which he wasn't), Irish and German (both of which he is) extraction – and alien Protestants. He is eldest son and third child of a large family deeply shaken when his father died shortly after his youngest brother's birth. His tendency towards contemplation grew from a sickly childhood, including two bouts of rheumatic fever that kept him in bed, sidelined to the company of books and his own imagination for several months each time.

Michael's adult ventures varied in almost everything except his unflagging dedication to social justice, community engagement and his family. His early journey to becoming who he is led through a seminary, two universities, a presidential campaign and community organizing in the poorest neighbourhoods of Chicago and Pittsburg. Then he moved to Canada where he continued his work in community organizing first in Toronto, then from a done-over mining town in northern Ontario, and then again when we returned to Toronto before moving here.

The return to Toronto was from a seven-year stint in Alberta that was Michael's first full-time immersion in writing. We moved to Alberta in 1975 when it was awash in oil money and investing heavily in culture. Michael was a favoured recipient of generous opportunity. He was mentored (and in turn was a mentor) through a government-sponsored correspondence course for writers overseen by John Patrick Gillese. Then at the Banff School of the Arts over the summer of 1976 the content of these stories was coaxed from Michael's sub-conscious. He slept all that summer in a tent, becoming the grizzled regular who educated newbies about being neighbours with bears, and clipped the meal tickets of his fellow students in the cafeteria. The following summer he was sent to a writing workshop in Antioch in Ohio, and the next year to Bread Loaf in Vermont, a prestigious gathering on the estate of Robert Frost, where he mingled with established and emerging writers of stature including John Gardiner and John Irving.

Michael is a gifted teacher. He first began adapting the freefall method he'd learned at Banff to teach farm women and university wives in space at the Camrose library bartered in exchange for janitorial services. When we moved to Calgary in 1978 he developed it further as a correspondence teacher for Alberta Culture, a continuing education instructor at Mount Royal College, a night class instructor for the Calgary School Board, and teaching juvenile offenders attending an Enviros wilderness camp (where he was ski-dooed in from where the road ended - a bit of an adventure for a city boy whose idea of a winter coat was to turn up the collar of his tweed sports jacket).

For the first year or two in Calgary, Michael had space at the Dandelion, an historic building at the confluence of the Bow and Elbow River where fledging artists of several mediums rented studio space for reasonable rates in keeping with the lack of insulation and ancient heating system. It was a hotbed of creativity, with emerging writers Edna Alford and Joan Clark publishing The dANDelion, a writers' magazine and organization that attracted the attention of Bill Kinsella on the cusp of celebrity, and Aretha van Herk who graced the parking lot with a white Porshe after winning the Seal First Author Award.

When the city sold the building for a more remunerative function, the literary elements of the Dandelion moved to the Alexander Centre, a city-owned recreational facility just down the street. Michael's adaptation of the freefall methodology flowered in fullness as he pulled people from all four streams of his teaching to become the first of generations of students at the Alexander Writer's Centre, founded in 1981. It is still a self-sustaining collective that continues to use this approach to produce an impressive roster of western writers.

Michael also invested in writing as a gifted organizer. He became active with PWAC (Periodical Writers' Association of Canada) in Calgary when he was writing magazine articles and book reviews. He was pressed into a second term as its president in 1989 and in that role was instrumental in inking Cancopy, now called Access Copyright. Michael then represented the interests of creators in negotiations with the international publishing world that took him to international meetings in Rome, Brussels, Berlin, Edinburgh, and bi-lateral meetings in London, Copenhagen, Paris, and Quebec.

Michael takes particular pride that he was successful in protecting 'orphan rights' so that members of recognized writers' organizations would share the income from the work of writers who could not be feasibly tracked. This provision was regrettably reversed in 2012. In the meantime, hundreds of millions of dollars were directed to writers who, like Michael, struggled to make a living from their craft. It was also appreciated by well-established writers; we have a lovely note from Robertson Davies framed on our wall: a properly typed formal expression of thanks that is circled by a postscript he added in his old-fashioned handwriting about his work being illegally copied and sold to students.

For almost twenty years Michael worked for the City of Toronto's Public Health department creating programs to serve a series of marginalized populations. When he retired from that work, he again devoted the meat of his days to writing. During his first decade in these northern woods he wrote plays. Six plays he wrote or co-wrote were produced, all rooted in the history and geography of this region in the context of larger conflictual forces – war, labor strife, settler solitudes. One, *Never Such Innocence Again,* was published in 2011 in a Theatre Ontario anthology, *Grassroots.* Michael also used his organizational skills to create and/or strengthen various local arts organizations and to make original theatre a participative art form in this community.

And then a few years ago Michael retreated deeper into his quiet office in this house in the northern woods. He opened that box of stories-awaiting-unconventional-length. And the work that led to their e-publication and now to this collection began.

Michael and I are delighted at the prospect of holding this collection as a bound book and giving it its designated spot on our shelves. I hope this introduction adds to your enjoyment of this long-tended dream realized.

Fay Martin
Minden, January 2018

The Whirlabout

1

As I turned the corner in the coming dusk and saw the marquee sparkling in the purpling light, it seemed like a magical talisman, pulling me into the world of movies.

I had no idea what film I was about to see. This was never the point in our house during the fifties. We went to *the movies*, not to any particular film. It was a period of great romantic comedies, with a new generation of young blondes replacing an older generation of exotic brunettes. Loretta Young became Doris Day; Myrna Loy became Connie Stevens. At ten, I didn't really know what was going on in those romantic comedies, but I did know I liked looking at those women on the screen, especially when colour began brightening their beautiful faces. And, as I skipped along, I was hoping hard to see those faces on such a pleasant evening in June.

I crossed the street, dug into my pocket, and stretched on tiptoes to slide my quarter to the girl in the ticket booth. She handed over a ticket with a dime in change. The theatre was wonderfully modern, with swirling silver shapes like those on the dashboard of our car, and multi-colored lights twinkling around the triangular marquee.

The door was always hard for a little boy to pull, but once inside, the tempting smell of popping corn and melting butter almost captured me. Instead, I decided to wait to spend my dime at intermission. Ushers, in fancy uniforms, holding flashlights with red extenders, were stationed at the top of both aisles. I didn't need their assistance to find my way to the third row and, as always, my aisle seat.

The mystery of the film I was about to see would soon be solved.

I did have a fear on those Friday nights. Horror films were the worst, but a close second were films about outer space invasions of earth. And on that night, one of my fears was realized.

The film opened with the landing of a flying saucer in a neighborhood that could be the very one I lived in, with sprawling maple trees, cozy streetlights, and tidy brick homes. After landing, the lights dimmed on the saucer and a troupe of gangly creatures came down a ramp, their bobble heads topped by antennas, as well as long and grasping arm-like appendages. The creatures crept into neighbourhood houses, sneaking past parents' bedrooms, and entering the rooms of the little ones. Little ones just like me. Children were taken from their beds after being put into a kind of semi-trance induced by a resonant humming that emanated from these creatures. Then the children were led into the flying saucer. Inside looked like the typical lab of a mad scientist, with gurgling vials of fluid, long lengths of clear plastic tubing, and a chair fitted with thick leather belts. One by one, the little ones were strapped to the chair, a needle was inserted in the crooks of their arms, and fluid flowed from the gurgling vials right into their veins. The effect was instant and dramatic. The little ones became completely robotic, controlled by sounds from the creatures, and sent back into their homes to take the lives of their mothers and fathers.

Why was Hollywood trying to terrorize me?

I couldn't watch anymore. I bolted from my seat and made my way to the concession stand, much to the surprise of the young man next to the popcorn popper.

"A bit early, aren't you?"

I quickly framed a boy's reply. "Hungry. Very hungry."

He scooped popcorn into a tall container, took my dime, and handed it to me.

"I think I'll eat it here."

I never did return to my seat, but rather stood in the well-lit lobby, slowly eating popcorn, kernel by kernel, until the movie was over and people began coming out to the concession stand. I realized at this point that, even though there were cartoons to come, I simply couldn't risk a return to my third row seat. I left.

Outside, the purple dusk had turned pitch black beyond the glow of the marquee. My task was to make it to the first of four streetlights on the way to my house. I hurtled into the pitch black, trying to keep my mind's eye occupied with what I hoped to see when I got home—my father, sitting on the couch with a bottle of beer, watching Edward R. Murrow. The race was on and, thank goodness, I made the first streetlight in record time. The light was thrown a few feet ahead of the standard and there was distance in the dark until the next one, but the dash was from splash of light to splash of light, not long enough for other images to tickle their way into my very active, always-in-motion, mind's eye. I reached the house, hammered up the porch steps, threw open the screen door, and tumbled inside.

My father was where he was supposed to be, eyes fixed on Murrow and Murrow's guest, slowly sipping on his bottle of beer. He didn't notice the feverish nature of my arrival and I settled onto the other end of the couch, so tempted to simply reach out and touch him, just to make sure he was actually there.

"Danny, can you get me a beer?"

He was there!

2

Cassie was on the other side of the ironing board, pumping a steaming iron over my father's white shirt, and, from time to time, looking up at me sitting on a stool watching her. She had a rich southern accent, with an almost Biblical intonation.

"It be hot down in the basin, boy not cool like up on this hill. It be hot down there. Why? I tell you boy. Nary a breath of air stirrin'. Nary a breath."

The hissing smell of white cotton sprinkled with starch rose up from the cuff of my father's white shirt. And her smell? Not like the smell of my grandmother, mother, or my four sisters no, it was gritty and urban and tinged with the sweat of a hard-working body.

Two large coal-burning furnaces heated our home in winter and smeared the walls and floor of the basement with a sheen of coal dust, creating an aura of dark, gritty mystery.

I became familiar with the raging fury of fire inside those furnaces when, after looking at naughty covers on the pocket books my grandfather, who lived on the second floor, bought by the dozens, I would hurl them into the inferno and watch them burn. All the while I believed it could be me burning, after being heaved into the hole of hell by the devil himself, if I kept looking at such trash.

Behind the furnaces on the far wall, were three small rooms. The one on the right was the door to the coal bin, piled high each fall with ragged chunks of coal dumped down the chute, which my father and I would shovel into the furnaces. The room next to that was much narrower and had no light. It was filled with the ancient, dusty detritus of my grandparents, parents, aunt and uncle. And finally, the third room attracted me, not for its purpose, but for some of the secrets it contained. My aunt and uncle didn't live long on the third floor, but while they were in the house, my uncle created a workshop with the kind of workbench, cabinets, and drawers you might find in a do-it-yourself magazine. There were tools, too, and a small red vise, but, more than the practical things I could never quite master, there were rolls and rolls of posters for cigarette, beer, and car companies, with exotic renderings of glamorous women. I would unfurl the posters and study the models and drift into worlds as wondrous as those in the movies. And, when I left the workshop, I often glanced at the furnaces, just to remind myself of the raging inferno that awaited me.

3

My father was spectacular to watch for his remarkable distinctiveness. He dressed every morning while wandering through our first floor apartment, starting in boxer shorts, a ribbed undershirt, black dress socks held up with men's garters, and black wing-tipped shoes. As he continued from closet to closet and mirror to mirror, he would add a freshly ironed white shirt and cufflinks, a blue silk tie with a carefully tied Windsor knot, and a pair of sharply creased suit pants. Along the way, he would have stopped in the kitchen for coffee and a Chesterfield. He never seemed to eat at that time of day. When he was ready to leave, he pulled on his suit coat, gathered up his debit book—a huge leather-bound book of records for insurance policies—and pause for one last look in the mirror by the door. The complete package always added up to irresistible masculine style. He looked like successful men you see on late night television shows.

"There!" he'd say. "Bye, my lovely. Be good to your mother, you kids."

And he'd be off, not to return until supper. When he came home, he would more or less reverse the dressing ritual, ending up in tan slacks and a black t-shirt, the embodiment of informal masculine style. He would play with us kids with great loving vigor, and was especially fond of lying on the living room floor to toss the little ones in the air till they rocked with raucous laughter.

His pulsing black Irish life force never seemed to let him down. He had a way with each of the children and a brilliant ability to know what each of us treasured. He would honor that with small gifts on the Fridays he was paid, and for me the gifts always revolved around my intense love of major league baseball. The love was epitomized in the boxes of baseball cards kept in the back of my closet in the bedroom.

My father added to that collection often, with a slickly packaged deck of ten cards and a slice of bubble gum. I would quiver with excitement each time I tore open one of those packages. There would be pieces of costume jewelry for the girls, and as they grew older, the costume jewelry would become real jewelry, pretty silver necklaces and handsome pins. The pinnacle of this tender child love was the yearly trip to a unique shoe store in his old neighborhood. He would orchestrate the choices of each of his brood and the owner would take all the time in the world, bring box after box until each of my father's children had exactly the perfect pair of shoes for the year to come.

4

THAT SUMMER I OFTEN sat quietly behind my father and our neighbor on the porch in the early evening, listening to their talk as they shared quarts of beer in brown paper bags, a baseball game playing on the radio in the background. I prided myself on my ability to ease into a state of almost invisibility as I watched and listened in on their world.

My father commanded the top step of the porch, his back resting against the brick archway. He wore his tan slacks and black t-shirt and his upper arms stretched the material with well-defined muscle. He had taken a sip from the quart of beer in the brown paper bag and handed it down to Big Ed. Our neighbor was just that—taller and broader than my father, with a wilder way of dressing on hot summer nights. He preferred loud shirts and reckless yellow pants. He took the beer from my father and, as usual, began a deep chug, this time taking the bottle down to the very last drop.

"Jesus!"

Big Ed slapped the empty bottle on the step as he looked at the sidewalk where Little Ed had stopped for a moment after crossing. Big Ed's son wore blue jeans and a white t-shirt. His short shirtsleeves were rolled up until they perched on his shoulders like baby doves. Little Ed was imitating the first baseman of our big league team, a man whose muscles were so enormous he had to cut off the sleeves of his uniform.

Crossing one gym shoe over the other, Little Ed revealed the rubber sole then tapped the sole with the handle of his baseball bat. Every single member of the big league team did the very same thing as he approached the batter's box for his turn at the plate. They tapped the dirt from their spikes, so when they stepped into the batter's box, they could dig out a fresh spot in the dirt with clean spikes to keep the back foot in place, improving their chances of hitting the ball solidly. Little Ed, of course, didn't have spikes on his feet, but was a majestic imitator.

"You Goddamn Knuckle-Head! What're ya doin with that bat?"

Little Ed wasn't the smartest boy on the block, but he was smart enough to never answer any of his father's questions that included, "Goddamn." And that night, showing real street smarts, he simply turned around and crossed the street again instead of joining us on the porch. Big Ed turned his attention to the empty quart of beer next to him. He picked it up.

"Whadda ya say, Chap?"

My father had that nickname since childhood and not a single soul called him by his real name—Willard. I only knew because that's how he signed my report cards.

"Another?"

'Why not," said my father.

And, like many other nights on the porch during those hot summers of the fifties, Big Ed made no move towards his back left pocket. My father only waited a beat or two before reaching into his own back pocket, pulled out his wallet, and drew out a dollar bill. Big Ed smiled and turned to me. I was chagrined my invisibility had been breached.

"Bruno-the Dog-Faced Boy," he said. "He walks and talks and crawls on his belly like a reptile."

Bruno, of course, was me. I had been Bruno to Big Ed for the past year or so. He was the instigator of occasional batting practice sessions in our driveway. My father would don the catcher's equipment he kept in a duffel bag in the garage, setting up at the rear end of the sixty-or-so foot driveway. Big Ed would take the pitcher's spot at the other end.

"Stay in there, Bruno," he'd bark. Winding up as a big leaguer would, he'd whirl his arms like windmills then let the ball go from behind his ear.

"It's okay, Danny," my father said.

But, as the pitch flew ever closer, angling towards my head, I would feel the harsh scrape of the side of the house against my back, as I scampered out of the way of the spinning white ball.

"Stay in there, Dog-Faced Boy!" Big Ed shouted from sixty feet away.

My father, usually a gentle and loving man, didn't intervene in these batting practice sessions.

But back to that night on the porch . . .

"Hustle down to Henry's," said Big Ed.

I knew enough to pop up immediately, not inviting any ridicule Big Ed might have in store for me. I took the dollar bill from my father and hurried from the porch to Henry's for their second quart of the night, happy not to have to say, "Charge it!"

5

MY MOTHER OFTEN SENT me to the stores in our little neighborhood. There would always be a note, even though I could have told the men and women what I needed, and there would always be my line, "Charge it!" I don't think I actually knew what that meant. I did know that, when I took a bottle of pills from the pharmacist and said, "Charge it!" he would rustle his forehead into wrinkles. Then he would move in slow motion to retrieve his ledger and begin to scribble in the amount, the wrinkles deepening. And, to complete the transaction, he would give me a glower that was the equivalent of a fastball to the head. I didn't like him.

The other storekeepers operated on a different basis.

I made almost daily visits to Sam the Butcher Man. Sam's was framed by a display case with cuts of meat, lined up almost like a colour chart: the browns of sausages, leading to the rich reds of lunch meats, to the pinks of beef, and finally to the near whites of pork. And, behind the display case, filling the entire length of the wall, was a painting of a farm, with green rolling hills, yellowing fields of grain, and cattle grazing behind a big red barn. The smells in the shop seemed raw and sweet, a symphony of differences united.

In the mornings of those summers gone by, my note would most often say, "Pound of ham sausage," and in the afternoons it might say, "Half dozen pork chops." And always, my line remained the same, "Charge it!"

"Okey, dokey," Sam would say. He was a huge presence in a white apron, splattered with the blood and muck of meat. He had a face the same shade as the cuts of honey ham in the display case, with round cheeks almost closing his small black eyes, as close as life gets to cartoons of little piggies. "Okey, dokey" seemed like a perfect response to me.

Country Maid Bakery was next to Sam's. The smell in the early morning was the unique blend of rock sugar on cream puffs just pulled from the hot oven. The smell seemed almost sacramental and, on the way home, would transform into the luscious taste of rock sugar on crispy brown pastry infused with cream. My mother never questioned the loss of that one cream puff, almost a tithe for her little boy's diligent loyalty. And the phalanx of white-haired, white-uniformed, white-shoed ladies never went rooting around for ledgers or sheets of paper to cover my quickly uttered, "Charge it!"

There was a second pharmacy in the neighborhood, just across from the bakery, but this place did as much trade in books, magazines, and comics as in drugs, cosmetics, and health aides. Sheridan's was my grandfather's favorite store on the street. The spiraling metal racks were filled with the newly popular pocket books with sensuous paintings of wild women with black hair and brilliant blue eyes, and of course, ample breasts bursting out of exotic dresses. My grandfather was a voracious reader of pocket books, which he would keep under the cushion of his reading chair on the second floor. I would sneak into my grandparents' apartment on the nights they were across town at a church bingo game, dig under the cushion, and devour as much of the book as time would allow. Like my almost miraculous ability to scrutinize and memorize baseball statistics, which bore no relation to my grade in arithmetic, my ability to read quickly and efficiently evolved into an almost genius-like ability to scan a page for 'trigger words' which would indicate that I should slow down and absorb a spicy scene.

There were also racks of magazines in Sheridan's. My grandfather was a major fan of any that had 'True' in the title: True Confessions, True Detective, True Romance, True, etc. I began associating the word 'True' with images of scantily clothed women pursued by men with black hair and pencil mustaches.

My grandfather, of course, never sent me to Sheridan's with a note and the instructions to "Charge it!" No, he took care of those purchases himself.

Mac's Barbershop was just around the corner from Sheridan's. Usually older men sitting in the three chairs, their faces slathered with shaving cream, waited for Mac to spin behind them, holding his freshly sharpened razor with the ancient pearl handle. The barbershop was always full of drawling voices of the men in the chairs, talking about matters far beyond my ken, like sewers and speed traps and crooked politicians. As I waited on one of the chairs along the wall under the massive mirror, I would rub the smooth skin on my chin, with no fear of the glinting silver weapon in the barber's hand. And a haircut was just a quarter, so no "Charge It!" to the man with the razor.

Dave's Hobby Shop featured plastic kits to build battle ships and jet planes, popular in the post-war era with boys my age, along with kits to build electric motors and telegraph sets that actually worked. Dave was a tall, gangly man with the deep reserve of a hobbyist. He always seemed to be tinkering with something behind the counter. I was just a looker at Dave's, never a buyer, and certainly not a charger.

The Deli next door had hard-to-get meats and cheeses, along with two rows of bottled and packaged delights that fathers enjoyed with their quarts of beer. My own father had a fondness for Limburger cheese, its nasty smell bursting from the fridge whenever the door was opened. He would add insult to injury by topping his cheese sandwich with onion slices and heavy brown mustard. The Deli owners were taciturn. I was fortunate in not being asked to 'pick up' items from their shop.

The bookends for the stretch of stores were the real centres of the community: St. Margaret's Church & School on the east and Roger Stern & Sons Funeral Home on the west, the Alpha and Omega of our lives. No "Charge It!" there.

6

But back to Henry's Pony Keg that July evening. Henry was a short man in bib overalls, a plaid shirt, and a beer company ball cap. The Pony Keg sold small kegs of local beers, but also sold beers by the bottle, wine, and spirits, along with a full range of snacks, with a heavy emphasis on various kinds of imported pretzels, a local favorite. Beer was bred in the bone in our community, with seven full breweries serving up a wide range of German-style lagers, pilsners, and bocks.

Henry seemed to truly enjoy me, relishing his tests of my knowledge of baseball statistics. I studied *The Sporting News* to prepare for these encounters. I kept abreast of batting averages, home runs, runs batted in, triples, doubles, most anything with a number and a ranking. As a dreamy boy in school, I could barely pay attention to anything the nuns tried to teach about multiplication or division, but when it came to baseball statistics, I seemed to soar to the level of an Einstein.

Henry looked closely at me from behind the counter that evening. I asked for the quart of beer for my father and Big Ed, but before giving it to me, Henry asked who was leading the league in home runs.

"Willie Mays," I said instantly.

Henry noted quite rightly that it was a very easy question, so he asked who was leading the league in doubles.

"Henry Aaron!" Of course, he preferred Henry to Hank.

Henry smiled at my quick, correct answer then swung around to open the large door of the walk-in cooler. He returned with the quart of Hudepohl Beer and slipped it into a brown bag.

"Charge it?" asked Henry.

"No, sir," I said, pulling the crisp dollar bill from my pocket.

"Regards to your Daddy," said Henry. "And I bet to Big Eddie, too."

I returned quickly to the porch, settled back into semi-invisibility and, with Big Ed and my father, listened to the announcer begin the baseball broadcast with a tribute to the sponsor. "The game tonight is brought to you by Hudepohl, the colden, golden lager!"

Big Ed held up the quart of beer and tipped it towards my father.
"Here's to you, Chap!"
"And you, Eddie."
"We should give the Dog-Faced-Boy some batting practice."
"Not tonight, Ed."
I hoped my sigh was inaudible.

7

Ralph Irwin was a former colleague of my father. He had left the insurance business and taken a management position in a factory nearer to his home. Ruby was his very good looking and intriguing wife. On visits that year, he seemed to look down on my father from his elevated position. But nonetheless, Ruby still laughed wonderfully and long at my father's humour and glanced at him in a certain kind of way.

Christmas that year was a typically joyous occasion in our house. With six children, most of them little, there was the heightened anticipation of Santa's arrival on Christmas Eve, the explosion of joy at finding presents under the tree, and the treat of playing with brand new toys on Christmas Day. This joy was shared the day after Christmas with relatives, friends, and colleagues. Ralph was sitting on a dining room chair in the archway between the living and dining rooms. Well dressed, he also sported an especially distinctive gold wristwatch. He had his eyes on Ruby who, as usual, had her eye on my father. At one point, the man got up, went to the closet, returned to his chair, and rested his heavy overcoat on his knees. The children scampered through the two rooms with a kind of Christmas abandon. Sue Ann, the youngest of my four sisters, was an adorable little girl, with shiny brown hair, eyes that sparkled with specks of blue, green, and brown, and a playful, sassy attitude. She had been wheeling in and out of the living room, smiling to herself, and, from time to time, breaking into sweet little giggles.

I saw Ralph take particular note of her. Most of the men my father worked with had very tiny families. This man had only one son and he was sickly. He always left him at home. I wonder if he thought one of us would give him germs.

Sue Ann wheeled into the room again, whirled around, and suddenly the man lifted the heavy overcoat from his lap, saying, "Catch, Susi!" He threw the coat over her, knocking her down like a tiny tree struck by lightening. Sue Ann began to scream in fright under the dark weight of the overcoat. The room was stunned and, for a long moment no one moved.

My father leapt up then and pulled the overcoat from his little girl.

"Just having a bit of fun, Chap," the man said with a snide tone.

My father looked at Ralph with clear, cold contempt in his eyes. He dropped the coat in Ralph's lap.

Sue Ann put her hands on her hips and filled the room with her sharp little voice. "You're just a big, old bully!"

The man stood up then, looked at his distinctive watch, and announced, "Let's go." He didn't wait for a response, but slipped into the overcoat and went to the front door and waited for his mortified wife to retrieve her coat from the closet.

"Merry Christmas," he said, then opened the door and they were gone. In a few beats the family recovered from the shock and sweet Sue Ann began to be her normal, carefree self again.

8

On hot, sticky nights at the end of summer, we often went to the Auto-In. My mother stayed home and appreciated the break from the gaggle of children. My father liked the privacy of watching a film while sitting behind the wheel of his Chevy, a quart of beer between his legs.

I remember one night more than any other.

I got into the front seat of the car, admiring the shiny silver curves of the dashboard. My father slipped in and turned the key, bringing soft green light to the radio dial. He pumped the clutch, shifted into reverse, and began backing out of the driveway. The other kids were cozily quiet in the back seat. He turned down the street and drove through the tunnel of old maple trees, past the yellow, orange, and red brick homes, then down the hill, where the homes were nicer and the landscaping careful. He turned at the bottom of the hill and headed towards the road that led to the Auto-In. After easing through the green light, he pulled into the parking lot of a small store. He returned in a moment with a brown bag wrapped around a quart of Hudepohl Beer. Our treats would come at the concession stand. We each had a shiny quarter from grandma to spend.

In a very short while, we saw the marquee for the Auto-In, emblazoned in a screen-sized rectangle of bright lights. My father pulled up to the small ticket booth, which sat halfway down the gravel entryway.

"Hi there, Chap."

"Hiya, Bill. I got all six kids tonight."

The man in the booth took the money from my father and hit a button that spit out seven tickets. My father pulled ahead and stopped next to another man, who wore a railway cap and carried a large flashlight.

"Hey, Chap. I saved your spot."

I loved hearing the words "your spot." The words represented a sense of order that appealed to me.

My father turned into the parking area. There were only a few cars at this early point in the evening, at least an hour before the film would begin. Looking ahead, I saw our spot in the very first row, right behind the playground, with swings, slides, teeter-totters, and, in the very centre, a whirlabout. After expertly pulling into our spot, Father took the speaker from the stand and hooked it on the lip of the window.

"Okay, kids."

I pulled on the handle and jumped out. My oldest sister flipped down the seat and the rest of the kids piled out, too. I let them scamper ahead of me. I felt the shiny quarter in my pocket and, seeing the light glowing from the concession stand, hurried there first. Visible through the small square hole in the front of the building, the giant reels of the film projector were ready to roll. The smell of popcorn came to me well before I reached the building, but I wasn't interested in popcorn. No. I'd invest my quarter in five, five-cent items, a tribute to the thriftiness that ruled my mother's side of the family. I bought Juicy Fruit, Juju Beads and a Tootsie Roll, saving two nickels for later, for the gumballs, trinkets, and treasures in the large glass container on the silver stand.

I hurried to the playground and, gliding one of the teeter-totters down to face the screen, lay on it, and ripped open the wrapper around my Tootsie Roll. The playground was not at all crowded, and my sisters and brother fell into their places. I looked up at the big white wall of cinder blocks. Soon the wall would be alive with colours, and sounds would pour from the dozens of speakers hooked on the lips of the car windows and all the children would settle into a favorite place to watch the cartoons. Later, we'd retreat to the car and watch the film through the windshield and smell the faintly pleasant aroma of beer as my father took the occasional sip.

It was all soothing, predictable.

I felt the cool hardness of the wood on my back and neck and began to bump my head gently on the wood, bump, bump, bump. I rested my hands on my stomach. A little boy sat in one of the basket swings, kicking his feet. A girl in the sandbox sifted sand through her fingers, digging deep, then brought sprays of sand to the surface. Another girl climbed up the slide, rushed down, bounced at the bottom, and ran around to climb again. The big swings were on the other side of the playground. The whirlabout sat between the two sets of swings, empty, a large circle of bars and boards, ready to spin.

I studied the big white wall of cinder blocks and began counting the rows: one, two, three, four, five . . . In my mind's eye, I was back in the driveway, facing Big Ed, and the ball was exploding from behind his ear again, like a tiny white rocket. Although I had known he would scream, and was worried what my father might think, I simply hadn't been up to it, so once again, I had quickly backed away from the rush of the ball.

I turned around and saw the Millers' car swing past the attendant. He was an old man; he once worked for the railway and handled his flashlight like he still worked for the railway, bringing trains safely into the yard. The Millers' car pulled into their spot, not far from ours.

I went back to counting the blocks of the screen, but my mind hurled ahead . . . I was standing in front of Big Ed again. He had a grin on his face, a mean grin, but suddenly and strangely I began feeling I might be on the verge of knowing what to do with Big Ed.

The Millers raced past me. Jeanne headed for the big swings and sat on one like it was a throne, posing as though she were an aristocratic lady. Jack headed for the slide, but stopped for a moment and gave the whirlabout a turn. Jack hammered up the ladder, then stood at the top of the slide and held his hands in the air, champion of the world.

The dark was falling now, the sky behind the screen was deep purple, leaves swished with the breeze which came up from the river, crickets sang, steady, sure, all around me. The film would start soon.

An old station wagon sidled past the attendant and snaked up and down the rows, looking for a spot. The car had low, fat tires, chrome hanging from the sides like splinters, and windows caked with mud. It must have come from the hills that circled the neighborhood. The loud muffler gurgled hoarsely behind me as I watched it move into the spot next to our car. The attendant would be mad the car took that spot. It was not part of the order.

The Whirlabout

I turned back to the screen.

A boy slipped by me like the light wave of a hand. I turned and saw the back door of the station wagon slam shut. The boy headed to the little slide, floated up the ladder, then whisked down, hopping at the bottom, bouncing up, and smiling a bright, warm smile.

He was wearing pajamas.

Running to the ladder again, he climbed, slid, bounced, smiled, looked at the boys and girls, and smiled again with a wider grin. But the others went on with their lazy swinging, their playing in the sand, carrying on like he wasn't there. The boy moved to the little swings. He held up the bar and tried to squeeze himself into the seat, but didn't fit. He ran across to the sand box and sat down, twirling sand with his fingers, looking up, smiling, but the children in the sand box ignored him, carrying on with their building, their sifting. He got up after a while and ran to the other side, to the big swings.

I turned and saw all the cars with their lights looking like eyes, wires dangling from windows, with the shadowy shapes of mothers and fathers wavering through windshields, talking, reading, waiting for the film to begin.

The door of the station wagon opened and the driver got out and turned to head towards the concession stand. He was wearing overalls and walked with a limp.

I looked back at the playground. The boy was on the big swings now, pumping his legs, swinging higher, his pajamas slapping and flapping in the breeze, and he was smiling, still smiling, a beaming, freckled smile, and he was looking at the big kids, smiling at them. But they, too, ignored him. He swung higher and higher, as high as anyone ever dared.

Jack and three other boys were whipping around on the whirlabout. The dust padded up from the running path around it, a circle of rising dust, and the boys squealed with the speed of the thing.

The boy in pajamas was still swinging, but had turned his attention to the whirlabout. His smile widened. The swing slowed down, he kicked at the dust to stop it, and each time a tiny burst of dust erupted when his bare feet hit the ground. The swing stopped. He hopped off and looked around the playground, looked at me, too, and his face was inquisitive now. The boy started for the whirlabout. He moved slowly, not gliding like before. He looked like an altar boy in procession, each step measured, his eyes straight ahead, his body under control. Jack rode alone now. The other boys twisted the thing around and around, beating up the dust in a rhythmic circle, almost like fog rising from the ground. The boy stood outside the circle with his hands at his side. The whirlabout went faster, faster, faster, and the boys jumped on one at a time, squealing, yelling, and the sound was guttural and primitive. Jack leaped off and raced around a turn and hopped back on again, quiet, riding, watching the boy, as though daring him to try.

The boy in the pajamas held out his hand and tried to grab one of the bars. The bar hit his hand and slapped it to his side. The boy backed away and watched the whirlabout. Jack hung over the side, still quiet, staring at the boy each time he passed him. The others were giggling, laughing, caught up in the sounds, the motion.

A horn blew, then another, and another.

I looked up at the big, white screen. A pale grey square appeared, then light, very light colours. The cartoon had begun. The horns stopped. The little kids danced away from the swings, the slide, the sandbox. I looked up at the cartoon, then down again to the whirlabout. The boy in the pajamas was standing there. The thing whirled around. Jack was quiet. The others squealed like wild animals.

It would happen, I just knew it.

Jack hopped off the whirlabout. He chased one of the bars, caught it, held it, pulling against it, moving forward, pulling back, slowly bringing it to a stop. The other boys watched him while they rode and waited. The whirlabout was still by then, the dust had settled down. Jack stood on one side, the boy in the pajamas on the other. The bars and boards were between them. Jack smiled, now. A sweet, sick smile, the kind you save for an aunt. The boy in the pajamas smiled, somehow more sweetly.

"Go ahead," said Jack.

The boy got on the whirlabout.

"All right," said Jack.

The Whirlabout

The other boys hopped off. Jack started to move the whirlabout slowly, trotting on the path, and it lilted around like a dream. The other boys helped out, one at a time, and it moved gently, easily. The boy rode around and around, his face beaming, eyes glistening. The boys on the path kept their eyes on the ground.

"Get pajama boy!" shouted Jack.

Jack began picking up the pace, the others speeding along with him. The whirlabout sped around, the dust rose up, and the boy grabbed the bar with his whitened fists. The whirlabout went faster, faster, faster, as the boys turned it, turned it, turned it. The boy held on, arched his back against the frantic spinning. He was just barely holding on, the boys were moving faster, faster. Pajama Boy seemed almost ready to fly off the whirling bars and boards.

I bolted, running to the whirlabout, my arms and legs pumping, my head pounding.

"Stop it!"

Jack darted away. The others disappeared into the lot, between the wires and the cars and the poles. I reached for the spinning bar, but as the boy flew past me, around again, and towards me now, there was a deep, animal sound as vomit exploded from his mouth, and stomach colours, slicing and spraying the circle, splattered on my clothes. I grabbed the bar, dug my feet into the ground, and stopped the thing. The boy sat, listless, grey, his eyes locked open wide. I reached for him, but he jumped down, fell, got up, fell again, got up and walked away in a dizzy, drunken trance to his car.

I stood, sick with the smell of vomit on me. I looked towards our car. My father was watching, his eyes fixed on me. I straggled over in a kind of slow motion, with all of what had just happened tumbling inside of me: the boy, the dust, the bits of food, the colours, all of it, tumbling, tumbling in my head. And what my father might think, might say.

I reached the car.

"That was brave, Danny."

"I guess it was."

Then I turned and saw the whirlabout turning, slowly, slowly, slowly.

"Yes, it was."

The Healer

THE RAIN CAME DOWN steadily as we stood under the soaring fly balls, the trees behind the backstop drooped with heavy rain. My T-shirt and pants were soaked, my hair dripping with unending wetness. The chill of the thick, wet grass rose through my canvas shoes and embraced my ankles. I was on the edge of a pack of boys in centre field, trying out for the parish baseball team.

One of the older boys had taken me under his wing. Pete was a snappy, cocky kid from an athletic family, and on the grass in centre field he moved like magic to settle under the white specks in the sky, pounding his glove, until the specks smacked into the pocket like meteors embedding in the earth. Pete had seen me making my way to the baseball field right after school and managed to pull me into his gang of guys. He was my mentor; I was a new altar boy. He led me out to centre field, but didn't set me up for embarrassment by pushing me out to try to catch one of those towering fly balls. He just allowed me to get the feel of being in centre field with the others, a kind introduction for an utter novice.

A novice in another way earlier that spring, I had taken training to become an altar boy, which was a requirement for eligibility to play on the parish teams. The nun in charge of the altar boys was a young, gentle-looking woman with wire-rimmed glasses, a sweet and resonant voice, and great patience in managing boys. She led several of us through the arduous task of learning the responses to the priest during Mass. We had no Latin in our regular curriculum so that language was a mystery. But the nun made me want to go to her classroom after school. I was happy to learn precisely how to say the Latin words and was ecstatic when she praised my ability to memorize the responses. She assigned me to Pete as a mentor and I served alongside him at Mass several times. I was delighted when this went smoothly. And my diligence was rewarded with permission to try out for the team.

After another dozen fly balls soared in the pouring rain, the coach called us in to the batter's box. I was first up at the plate. The pitcher was tall with square shoulders and a long, supple pitching arm and the motions of a pro. Facing our neighbour Big Ed the summer before had taught me that those motions could be hypnotic. I'd developed the confidence to keep my eye on the ball, not the motions of the pitcher.

The pitcher wound up. On that rainy day when the ball appeared suddenly from somewhere behind the pitcher's ear and seemed to be sailing directly for my head, I held my ground. I swung as the curveball broke toward the centre of the plate. Perfect timing. The ball cracked off the bat and, magically, sailed right over the pitcher's shoulder. He collapsed in a heap.

Pete's voice broke into the sudden stillness. "Way to go, Danny! Way to go!"

The euphoria didn't last. I was soon staring at my swollen, throbbing ankles set in an enamel bowl of lukewarm water and Epsom salts. My mother was at the Formica table with an anguished look on her face, her hands clasped on the shiny, marbled surface. Marge and Beth, my older sisters, were washing and drying the dishes. Daddy was away on a business trip and his absence was written large all over my mother's face.

"Maybe we should phone the doctor?" she seemed to be asking my absent father.

"It's okay, Mom."

"I just don't know."

"It's really okay."

"I'm phoning," she said.

A brief phone call led to an immediate visit to the pediatrician's office at the bottom or our street. A thorough examination, with a pinprick on my middle finger to draw blood, led to a tentative diagnosis of strep throat.

"Strep throat?"

"Yes, Mrs. James."

I was sitting on the examining table wearing shorts and a T-shirt and my ankles looked like bulging sweet potatoes.

"Doesn't that have to do with rheumatic fever?"
"Sometimes it does, Mrs. James."
"Oh, I wish Chappy were here."
"He's away?"
"He's on a week-long sales trip."
"I see. How about we admit Danny to hospital to run some tests for rheumatic fever."
"Is there a choice?"
"We have to be very careful about permanent damage to the heart if it's rheumatic fever."
"I'm aware of that. My brother had it. He died eventually."

～

THE SMELL IN THE CHILDREN'S ward was a peculiar combination of harsh cleaning fluid and medicines, laced with the faint odour of antiseptic swabs that were used for the seemingly endless drawing of blood to determine my red blood cell count. A low count would be a key indicator of rheumatic fever. The shallow draws came from the tips of my fingers, sometimes with a pinprick, sometimes with a razor slash. The deeper draws reminded me of how the little ones suffered in the lab of the flying saucer in a movie I once saw by accident. They were strapped down by gangly creatures, injected with a serum, and sent back to kill their mothers and fathers. Not a nice memory under the circumstances.

The nurse tapped a vein in the crook of my left arm to make it rise then inserted a hypodermic needle attached to a glass cylinder. These draws were conducted by a rotation of nurses, on the instructions of a rotation of doctors, accompanied by a never-changing line of encouraging dialogue: "Be a big boy." Ironically, I would never "be a big boy." As a matter of fact, I remained the smallest child in the school well into grade two and even in later grades; I was always the smallest child in the class. "Be a big boy" wasn't the right rallying cry.

Daily, groups of men in white coats circled my bed, usually one older man leading a number of younger ones. I learned that the older doctors were specialists and the younger were residents or interns. I also noted that the younger men seemed to think with their right hands cupping their jaws. If the thinking called for a word or two, the right hands dropped and the left hands began to gesture. The gestures were almost like bits of punctuation: commas, periods, exclamation points. The questions stopped when the specialist unfurled the stethoscope from around his neck. This meant that my hospital gown would be untied and pulled down to reveal my narrow, naked chest. And the stethoscope would meet my skin, causing a sudden unpleasant chill to ripple through my body. The shiny silver circle wandered around the general area of my heart then, when I turned as told, wandered around between my shoulder blades. The specialist handed off the procedure to the first intern or resident, who followed the same path with a freshly chilled silver instrument, followed by another and another and another. And then the specialist drew a small rubber-tipped hammer from a back pocket and, pulling the gown above my knees, began an almost ritual tapping that, at one point, caused my leg to jerk to attention. This hammering went through the herd of interns and residents, one by one, until my knees gave up and refused to straighten the legs on command.

These roving bands in starched white coats ended their visits by scribbling on the chart hanging at the foot of the bed. I began to realize that the scribbling eventually meant another visit from a nurse with a hypodermic and glass cylinder, saying sweetly, "Be a big boy."

I spent a lot of time looking out the window above my bed and down on the parking lot below me, with its swinging entry gate, and beyond that to a broad boulevard, quite the biggest I'd ever seen. And further, an endless sea of dark green trees in the twilight, rolling into the distance—a park certainly, but I didn't know the name. The other boys who shared the room had me wishing I could somehow squeeze myself through the window and escape to the safety and comfort of the green blanket of trees beyond the boulevard.

One boy was frighteningly ugly. A toddler in a crib, the top of his head had been opened for some reason then sewn back to the bottom half with zigzagging black thread. When I saw it the first time, I couldn't help but see my grandma with her large darning needle working on one of my grandpa's socks, piercing the material then pulling the thread through. I imagined in an instant that somewhere in this huge hospital there must be a room where such sewing happened. The boy could only burble like my little brother, with just two words at his command: "My mine." This referred to a small blanket that never seemed to leave the clutch of his tiny hands.

At times he would pull himself up with those tiny hands and stand there, looking at the other boys, his bald scalp blotched red where the threads went in and out. I felt terrible that I had a hard time looking at him. Visitors never came to see him. He was taken from the room every day and brought back, dressed in a clean hospital gown. The nurses never tried to talk to him, but the young volunteers who came in the late afternoon always said, "Hello." And a few times, a volunteer would gurgle baby-talk things she might have learned from a younger sibling. He didn't cry like a normal baby; the sound he made was more like the whimper of a small, hurt animal. One day, he did not return to the room and for me the empty crib became harder to look at than the toddler had been.

The boy next to him was caught up in a contraption of wires and pulleys, with casts on both his legs and another on his left arm. Ben spoke with that hold-the-vowel drawl that seemed to rise from the green hills on the south side of the river. He told me he'd fallen from the roof of a barn. The contraption squealed whenever he strained to move his plaster-bound legs, and the wires would sway with the squealing. He was a pleasant boy, talked quietly with his visitors, never pestered the nurses. Like me, he grimaced when we were confronted with the bedpan in the morning, afternoon, and evening. He seemed to have a great capacity to hold whatever he'd eaten, sometimes for days at a time, and the nurses frowned a scolding when they looked at the bottom of the obviously empty bedpan. When no evening visitors came to see him, Ben would sleep soundly through the night.

And opposite him, separated from me by a small table, was the boy who moved me the most. Sammy was also from the south side of the river and spoke with the same lilting, lovely drawl, complete with a kind of internal rhythm that came from living deep in those green rolling hills. Of all of us, he was the most tragically ill. He said he could barely contain the pain when it suddenly shot through him. He would react as if he had been struck with a leather whip, with a whelping sound that was frightening, and then he slipped into a continuous moaning he could not seem to stop. There was nothing the many doctors, interns, and nurses could do to ease that pain.

One night Sammy's world closed in on me.

~

As I looked through the window to the park across the street that night, a blue and white bus pulled away from the bus stop and, there, by the row of red tulips, wearing a tan spring coat, was my mother. I turned from the window and inhaled the sharp, medicinal air. The boy in traction was fast asleep. The boy in the next bed rustled in his sleep, tumbling on his stomach, revealing his narrow back, then curled into the sheets like a small animal. After a while, I heard heels clicking in the hall, and my mother came into the room. She sat down next to me and smiled.

"How are you, honey?"

"I'm fine, Mom."

She looked at the boy in the other bed. "How is he?"

"He's fine, Mom."

"He's very sick, you know. The nurse said it was leukemia."

"I know, Mom. Sammy told me."

She leaned close to me.

"He should be in a private room."

"Why?"

"He should, Danny."

"He'd be lonely."

I turned away from her. The boy in the other bed was curled into a round, soft ball. My mother continued to chat, with news of my sisters and brothers, my grandparents, and my father's sales trip. But she also glanced from time to time at her watch. After a while, she opened her purse and pulled out a paperback book.

"Eddie dropped over with this. Do you like crosswords?"

"No." The word was as sharp as the slash of the razor.

She stood up and went to the window. "I can only stay for a few more minutes, honey. I left the kids with grandma. But I wanted to see how you were."

"I'll be okay if you go, Mom."

"I'll come back tomorrow," she said. "Daddy will be back, too. He's dying to see you."

My mother came to the bed and kissed me on the forehead.

"Bye, Mom."

"I'll be back tomorrow. And thank God your father will be with me."

She straightened her back, smiled sadly, and walked out of the room.

I grabbed the post of the bed and pulled myself into the window. The park was purpling now, rolling like a dark dream toward the river. The guard gate in the parking lot lifted and a car moved into the traffic on the street. After a while, a small figure came out of the entrance and stopped—my mother. She crossed the street and joined the clutch of people waiting at the bus stop. A blue and white bus pulled up to the curb, filled up with people, and was gone. I pressed my nose against the glass and felt the coolness.

"What're you doing?"

I dropped down into the bed. The nurse stood in the doorway with her hand on her hip. She held a small tray in her other hand. She swung into the room and set two cups of juice on the table between the beds. I quickly drank mine. She looked at the boy with leukemia.

"Has he been sleeping long?"

"Since supper."

"He sleeps when he should talk and talks when he should sleep."

She went to his bed and, with her free hand, deftly pulled the sheet over the boy's shoulders. Then she turned and disappeared into the dark hallway. Sammy kicked at the sheets and rolled back and forth. He opened his eyes.

"What time can it be?"
I said nothing.
"Your Mama been here?"
I said nothing.
"You be sleepin'?"
"No," I said.
"I didn't think so. I knew you'd be with me. I just knew."
The boy sat up, pale eyes foggy with sleep.
"I had me a dream, I did. You wanna hear her?"
I turned my head away from him.
"She was real good, she was."
"Okay," I said.
Sammy slid to the side of the bed and sat up, dangling his legs.
"She was about him. I knew him from his voice. I heard him, with my grandma, hundreds of times on the radio."
"Who?"
"The Healer."
"What happened?"
"He came in here and touched my head and I felt a great heat from his hand and I got up and flew out of this place and away down by the river."
"Where?"
"Away down to my grandma's. She was on the veranda waitin' for me, wearin' the same dress she was wearin' on the day they took me away, and she opened her arms and I flew into them and I was home and, Praise the Lord, I was healed."

Sammy stared ahead blankly. He seemed as thin as a slat of wood. He began to shiver. He wrapped his arms around himself and lay down and spread his arms wide and closed his eyes.

The nurse came into the room again.
"What's he been doing?"
"Nothing," I said.
"Then why is he lying there like he just ran around the block?"
"We were talking."
"Was he talking about that healer again?"

The boy opened his eyes. "I'm not sayin'."

The nurse sighed.

"This talk of healing should stop. The only healing's been done, already's been done. A long time ago. The Lord's been gone a long time, and there's no more healing."

"My grandma told me."

"Your grandma don't know nothin' about healing."

"She told me and she don't lie."

"She don't come and see you either, boy."

"She's old and she can't come."

The nurse turned to me. "I want you to mind me. It's time for you boys to go to sleep now. You hear me?"

"Yes, ma'am."

"I just want you boys to be good and get well and get on home."

Sammy sat up in the bed. The nurse picked up the cup of juice and handed it to the boy.

"She don't lie," he said.

The nurse left the room. The boy drank the juice and threw the small cup on the floor. His pale grey eyes stared into the darkening hallway.

"She don't believe," he said. "My grandma told me that them that don't believe are the work of the devil. The devil sends 'em here to take us into the fires of hell so we can burn and our skin can boil and our blood can break from our veins. The Healer told me, too."

"He did?"

"He did, Dan. I heard him on the radio. I was there in my bed in the kitchen. My grandma was there with her knittin' needles. The radio was on and then he comes on and starts in talkin'. He talks about the pigs and the cliff. He talks about them snortin' and spittin' and rammin' into each other, bangin' their heads, screamin' like a million babies, and then runnin' and throwin' themselves over the cliff, smashin' on the rocks, heads breakin' open and spillin' brains. All because of the devil."

"And the nurse is a devil?"

"She is. Now, she don't know it. They never do. He gets in you and there's nothin' you can do about it."

"I know one of them."

"She got the devil?"

"No. She does the ironing because my mom can't."

"She must believe then."

"Yeah. She must believe."

The boy lolled his head to the side. His eyes were as pale as parchment. "I'm gonna lay down." He slumped into the sheets.

"Sammy?"

"Yeah, Dan?"

"Will he heal anybody?"

The boy sat up straight. "He can heal anybody who needs healin'."

"Could he heal me?"

The boy slipped across the narrow space between the beds. He sat down on my bed. He seemed to float on the surface of the sheets.

"Could he come here?"

"He could, Dan. He could come if we put our minds on him. He'll come like he come in my dream. He'll come and touch us and heal us. Why, if he can heal me with my leukemia, he can sure heal you with your rheumatic fever. And then he'll take us on home."

"How do you put your mind on him?"

Sammy's eyes were as soft and luminous as the eyes of a saint.

"I blank everything from my mind. I listen. I listen and listen and listen. I hear him then. I hear the words."

"You hear them?"

"I do. I hear those words. I can't see him like I see him in my dream, but I hear those words. He promised all the sick and all the dyin' that he'd come in their hour of need. This is my hour. My grandma told me to put my mind on him and he'd come and he'd heal me and he'd take me on home."

"Will he heal a Catholic?"

"He'll heal anybody who needs healin'. He don't mind for religions. I can see the believin' in your eyes. He'll come and heal us and take us away. I just know it."

The boy reached out and touched me on the hand. The boy's hand was hot.

"Sammy!"

The boy jerked his hand away.

"What are you doing out of your bed?"

The boy turned around slowly. "We were talkin'."

"You get back in your bed."

The boy stood and slipped across the floor to his own bed. The nurse came into the room and stood between us with her arms folded across her chest.

"I'm ashamed of you both." She looked at me. "I thought you were a good boy."

I said nothing.

"I thought you were a boy who could talk some sense into Sammy."

The nurse turned to Sammy and softened.

"I'm sorry for saying such a mean thing about your grandma."

The boy said nothing.

"I just want to help you get better. I don't think it's good for you to believe all this about healing."

"She don't lie," said Sammy.

The nurse turned and slowly walked away. She switched off the light.

"I'm gettin' some rest now, Dan. I'm sure he'll be comin' soon."

I lay in the dark for a while, listening to the descending hush in the hospital. I reached for the table between the beds and picked up my rosary. The beads were cool in my fingers. I laid the rosary down, grabbed the bedpost and pulled myself up to the window. The darkness was heavy and thorough, only broken by the pale street lights along the avenue. I slumped down into the bed again. The room was quiet and the air was sharp, medicinal. I closed my eyes and drifted off, approaching sleep. A rustling broke into the silence. A quick whelp led to moaning, moaning.

"I got the pain!"

I opened my eyes and lifted myself on my elbow. I could see the pale figure in the other bed, jerking this way and that.

"The pain is in me!"

I reached around and grabbed the cord and pulled it through my fingers. I clicked the switch and the red light above the door went on.

"Sammy?"

The boy said nothing.

"Sammy?"

The boy was a still, silent shape in the bed. I tried not to think what that might mean. I wanted to get up and go to him and touch him, but, like so many moments since coming to the hospital, I knew what had happened.

The nurse rushed into the room. The light suddenly went on. The traction entangling the other boy began to squeal in the deathly silence.

"He's got the pain!"

The nurse circled the boy's wrist with her large hand. She dropped the wrist, soundlessly, and ran from the room. The boy was white and still in the bed. An orderly rushed in and stopped for a second then drew the curtain around the boy's bed. A nurse came into the room. A tall, thin physician behind her. I heard the hollow thumping behind the curtain, over and over, and sharp, medical words. Then I heard nothing.

"That's it," a man's voice said, coldly.

The curtain was ripped away. A horrible squeal sounded and, in one quick motion, the bed was gone.

The room was white and sterile. The nurse returned and came to my bed. She sat down and was like a dark mountain above me.

"I'm sorry," she said.

"He's dead?"

"He's gone to the Lord."

"No."

"Yes, my boy, he has. Try and go to sleep now."

As the nurse turned to walk away, I wanted to reach for the rosary and fling it wildly at her wide back with an anger that was somehow in my very soul. But I didn't.

"What's going on, Danny?" said Ben. I couldn't find my voice to answer.

"He's dead, isn't he?"

My voice was far away, not to be found.

"I'm gonna pray on him, Danny. Pray with me?"

The Healer

I reached for the empty cup on the table and threw it on the floor where Sammy's cup lay. And suddenly I felt terribly alone in the cold, medicinal room.

～

After the two weeks I spent in the hospital, I was bedridden for the rest of the summer and tried to find ways to keep myself amused. My routine became a round of nights in the Little Room, sleeping in a rented hospital bed; mornings in the living room with the television or on the porch lying on the chaise longue with the *Sporting News*; and evenings in the living room with my father for the late-night television shows. I was a tiny boy so my mother was able to carry me back and forth to the bathroom.

I quickly became addicted to watching a morning talk show that was filled with an eclectic combination of interviews, recipe testing with an assistant, music from the studio band, and incredibly intimate chats with the audience. The set was arranged to look like a living room, with a couch and two wing chairs. Ruby White, the hostess, used a hand-held microphone adorned with a small bouquet of fresh flowers. I enjoyed interviews with visiting celebrities such as Jerry Lewis and Tony Bennett, who appeared at nightclubs just across the river from our house.

Ruby would settle on the couch, hold the microphone with tenderness, look right into the camera, and talk in an intimate and revealing way about her family. She was married to a professor who only appeared on the show once a year around Christmas time. He was a plain man with spectacles who looked a bit like my accountant uncle. He seemed, to my young mind, a fairly preposterous choice of partner for this glamorous hostess, whose job it was to charm handsome and famous men. She also talked about her daughter who was in the early grades of high school and, favouring her father, was a plain and deeply shy girl who always seemed uncomfortable during her once-a-year appearance. The hostess would go on and on about them, however, making the plain and ordinary details of their lives seem somehow magically touched by her glamour.

Ruby would also lead her audience in singing her own Christmas song:

> *It's four more months till Christmas,*
> *Four more months till Christmas,*
> *Four more months till Christmas,*
> *And Santa will be here.*
>
> *And don't forget the children,*
> *The poor deserving children,*
> *Don't forget the children,*
> *Who'll have no Christmas cheer.*

I hummed along with that song in front of the television. I couldn't get it out of my mind that there were actually children who would "have no Christmas cheer." When my mother caught the show one day on the way from one chore to another, she mentioned that the toy area in the children's ward at the hospital where I had spent two weeks was a gift from the program. I was stunned. Was I one of those "poor deserving children"?

The other kids in our family went to bed fairly early those summer nights and my mother did, too. Daddy and I ritually watched a nightly national talk show hosted by Steve Allen. He and my father could have been brothers. They were compact and sturdy, impeccably dressed, and had black hair and black-rimmed glasses. And their magnetic laughs, deep and resonant, engaging, were hard to resist. The two men began to mesh in my mind: both handsome, both snappy dressers, both the life of the party. I felt privileged to spend so much time in the midnight hour with my two favourite men, Chappy and Steve.

And I had another great thrill, night after night. At a certain point, during one of the commercials, Daddy would turn to me and say, "How about a sundae?" I would always nod. He'd go into the kitchen, dig out the ice cream, pour on the chocolate sauce, and, in a New York kind of gesture, sprinkle a handful of nuts on each chocolate-covered mountain.

∼

LATER IN THE SUMMER, I was on the chaise longue on the front porch by myself. My mother was down in the basement with the laundry and the five other kids were out and about in the neighbourhood. The fullness of summer was before me through the arch of the porch, with the two giant maples on the street edge bursting with great green leaves. I had the *Sporting News* on my lap and was doing my weekly scan of batting averages for the big-league season. I was about as content as any eleven-year-old with rheumatic fever could possibly be.

The screen door swung open. Bobby hopped down on the porch, wearing his favourite shorts-and-shirt set, red with a white sailboat on his tiny chest. Bobby was the only child who took completely after my father. He had thick black hair and dark brown eyes, while the rest of us had brown hair and eyes in various shades of blue. Bobby was also the sweetest and quietest of the children. He smiled constantly at the wonder of the world around him. As usual, he only gave me a glance and a little smile, but didn't say a thing. Wearing his tiny black sandals he skipped ahead then and hopped down the cement steps. Instead of turning toward the driveway, he skipped down the sidewalk dividing the front lawn into two perfect rectangles. My attention strayed away from the numbers in the paper. I felt a surge of joy watching that little boy in red skipping through the summer frame of green trees and grass. When he reached the sidewalk in front of the house, instead of heading down the street, he scooted to the patch of dirt between the sidewalk and the street. My father and my grandfather had spent many springs trying to get grass to grow on that patch of dirt, but it never amounted to more than a few anemic sprouts that disappeared as spring turned to summer.

I heard a car rushing down the street and bolted to attention when it screeched to a skidding stop. Smack! Bobby went down, his head cracking on the pavement, blood spilling from his forehead. My body was stuck to the chaise longue, my voice frozen deep within my chest.

With cinematic clarity I saw the two people in the car gesturing and speaking frantically. Then in a flurry of movement, the man suddenly jerked behind the wheel and the woman slipped into the passenger seat.

"Mom!" I finally found my voice. "Bobby's hit!"

I remained stuck to the chaise lounge as if strapped to it by thick leather belts.

"Mom! Bobby's hit! He's there!"

The screen door slapped open.

My mother tore down the steps, raced to the street, and swept Bobby up in her arms. She ran down the street toward the pediatrician's office.

The man and woman, still in the car, continued to gesture and talk like a film in fast-forward.

"They switched," I said to myself.

I stared at the car while the man rammed it into gear and pulled away. A green 1955 Chevrolet with whitewall tires. I strained to catch the license plate. Fortunately, a vanity plate; easy to see and remember. But I still wrote it in the margin of the paper on my lap.

A little later my father pulled into the driveway. He got out, waved quickly, and hurried down the street the way my mother had gone with Bobby.

I waited and waited, wondering and worrying. After a long while, my mother and father came back with Bobby. My mother carried him carefully in her arms. A bandage hid Bobby's forehead, but amazingly, he was smiling. While my mother took Bobby into the house, my father sat down at the foot of the chaise longue.

"Tell me what happened, Danny." His voice was warm and comforting.

I told the whole story, the details still precise in my mind's eye. I told him about Bobby skipping, the screeching car, my baby brother slapped to the asphalt, and the blood.

"They switched, Daddy!"

"What?"

"The woman was driving, but when they hit Bobby, the man jerked behind the wheel."

"Are you sure?"

"I'm positive."

"And then what?"

"He just drove away."

My father looked like he had been hit in the stomach.

"But I know the car, Daddy."

"Tell me."

"It was a 1955 Chevrolet with whitewall tires."

"Good, Danny."

"And I wrote down the license plate."

"You did good, Danny. That means they won't get away with this."

"I hope so, Daddy. They were bad people. They didn't care that they hit Bobby."

"They may not be bad people, but they did a real bad thing. People have to own up for what they do."

"Daddy?"

"What, Dan?"

"Am I a bad person because I didn't take care of Bobby? I should have stopped him from running into the road."

My father leaned close and laid a firm hand on my thin shoulder.

"You know you're not to go off the chaise. That's your job now and you did it well. And you used your sharp eyes and your sharp brain to do what was needed. You did good, Danny!"

The steadiness of his hand on my shoulder told the truth of his words.

That night my mother slept in the room I shared with Bobby, and my father carried me to their bed. I had a hard time settling down. I watched him curl his arms around his pillow, instead of putting it under his head. He explained to me how wonderful it was to have the pillow to hug at night, no matter what had happened during day, to feel the soft coolness and, with that, he fell into peaceful sleep. And, like him, I did the same.

∽

My father took special care when dressing for trips to insurance-company conventions, and made a final stop at the closet in the Little Room before he was finished. Daddy's suits hung in the closet. I had spent two-and-a-half months convalescing in that room after suffering with rheumatic fever the previous summer, but now it had been returned to its original function as my grandmother's office for her work with the Ladies Catholic Benevolent Association. She once took me to one of their monthly luncheons in a fine restaurant across the river. I remember the sheer pleasure of eating sugar cubes and stabbing tiny triangles of pineapple with red-ribboned toothpicks. The Little Room looked out on the two large maples in the front yard through an ornate multi-paned window.

Daddy had rifled through the closet that early evening and, among the business suits in shades of blue, black, and charcoal, found his new grey summer suit. He stood now in front of the mirror next to the closet, with the pants in one hand. He had gone through his usual ritual of dressing, walking from place to place in the apartment, and carefully examining his reflection in the mirror: a starched white shirt, a patterned blue silk tie with a perfect Windsor knot, boxer shorts, male garters, long and elegant navy blue socks, and the inevitable black wingtip shoes. When he pulled on the pants and slipped on the coat, he looked magnificent.

"There!" he said. "Okay, kiddos! Are we ready?"

We had all assembled by the luggage at the front door. My mother wore a fresh sky-blue dress and clutched her favourite purse.

"We're ready, Daddy!" I tried to be first off the mark in these exchanges and waited for the echo of my five siblings.

"We're ready, Daddy!"

We helped with his luggage, piled into the car, and rode with great anticipation to Union Station. The massive building was shaped like a dome, with a long circular driveway leading to the front entrance. When the car was parked, we jumped out and pulled the luggage from the trunk and the whole family trekked through the massive front doors.

A symphony of sounds and sights met us. The train master called destinations and tracks: "New York City, Track 1; Detroit, Track 2; St.

Louis, Track 3." Men hustled to catch their trains, women studied the huge arrivals board, and children squirmed on the circular benches.

Above all this, gigantic murals spanned the entire arc of the ceiling: images of working men firing furnaces, pounding iron, scaling the ribs of skyscrapers; bold, dramatic men in deep colours, with faces so real they almost seemed able to speak to the tiny humans below. As I craned my neck to stare at them again, I wondered who these men really were, the houses they lived in, who their families were—all the real-life questions that somehow brought their huge majesty down to a human scale.

Trips to the train station magnified the significance of my father, knowing he was a man who traveled to places I only knew of as baseball teams in the sports pages of the paper.

My father had already visited one of the ticket booths and bought a round-trip to Detroit. Then we all followed him to Gate 2. A good-sized group of men in business suits was waiting by the entrance. My father first greeted four others from his office then returned to his own entourage. He gave Mom a hug, and crouched down to the size of Susi, the smallest of us, and waited for the rest to circle around him under the great mural overhead.

"Susi, what will you be when Daddy's gone?"

"I be good, Daddy!" She was quick and bright, and her blue eyes shone. Daddy looked around at the rest of us.

"And you?"

"We'll be good, Daddy," I blurted. And not to be outdone, I added, "And we'll take care of Mom!"

The kids repeated both blurts.

My father rose to his full height, pulled the ticket from a breast pocket, and picked up his briefcase and thick debit book.

"Okay," he said. "I gotta go."

"Goodbye, Daddy!" The chorus was quick and unanimous.

"I'll see you in one short week."

He kissed my mother then, along with the other men at the gate, disappeared down the deep steps to the train tracks.

The week went by like the wind that spring of 1957. As always, it was hard for me to pay attention to Sister Antoninus droning on about long division, so, when I looked at the fresh blossoms bursting outside the schoolroom windows, I let my imagination and memory go wherever it wanted to go.

One afternoon, almost in a deep trance, I remembered having gone to church with my father the Sunday before he left for the convention. He enjoyed taking me to the old and somewhat shabby church he had attended as a boy. On that warm spring morning, we drove down the western hills to the black neighbourhood in the basin of the city, located the soot-covered bell tower, and parked the car in front of the church. A young black boy emerged from somewhere and said, "Watch ya car, sir? Watch ya car?" My father dug into the pocket of his trousers and pulled out a handful of shiny silver coins. The boy's face lit up like magic. "Oh, I watch it now, sir. I watch it good." I was so proud of my father in moments like these!

Then we went inside. The shabbiness of the building was sad. However, beneath the wear and tear, the soot and dirt, there was real marble on the floor and the altars. And the stained-glass windows glowed with a kind of spiritual wonder. We sat near the back, where we could see the sweep of the entire black congregation. I had been an altar boy for over a year by then, so I was able to follow the sequence of the Mass from an insider's point of view. I slipped into deep concentration, rolling the responses off in my mind, watching carefully how these black altar boys fulfilled their roles in the ritual. My father seemed to decompress in his childhood church in the basin, moving into the same kind of trance I did by the window in my classroom.

When we returned to the car after Mass, my father shook the appointed car-watcher's hand. As we drove back up the hill toward home, we talked about somehow fixing up the church, bringing back the magic of the time when my father sold newspapers on the corner of Eighth and State to men getting off the old streetcars after a day's work in the machine shops in the river valley. I found these dreams shared with my father the most magical feature of all in my life.

When the week of the convention was over, my mother drove us down to Union Station to pick up my father. On the trip home from the station, he broke into a song that often came from the silver speaker in the dashboard of our car. I listened in the back seat with my sisters, a smile on my face. My father really sounded like the crooner he was accompanying.

> *When the moon hits your eye,*
> *Like a big piece of pie,*
> *That's amore!*

When my father repeated the verse, he deliberately stopped after the first line. I took the cue and, taking a deep breath, followed with the next two lines:

> *Like a big piece of pie,*
> *That's amore!*

When a few more alternating lines took us to the end of the song, I gathered even more courage.

"Daddy? I sound like Eddie Fisher, don't I?"

My father didn't take but a moment to reply.

"That's so, Danny. That's so."

My heart soared in a moment of sheer triumph.

My oldest sister, sitting by the back-seat window, rustled indignantly.

"You do not sound like Eddie Fisher!"

I didn't risk saying the words out loud, but they rang in my ear like a clarion call: "If Daddy said, 'That's so,' by golly, that's so!"

There was great excitement when we arrived home, with the whole gaggle of us children gathered eagerly around the dining-room table, all the bulbs in the chandelier burning brightly while we waited for Daddy to open his suitcase. He had the amazing knack of finding something wondrous for each of us. I remembered one of mine from another convention—a hand-held slide projector with a circular set of slides of the major league stars. I waited patiently under the chandelier for my turn.

My father would at times cleverly recruit those bright bulbs into his dressing routine. If the socks he required to match the suit of the day were not quite dry from the previous day's laundry, he would slip them over the bulbs, flick the switch on and, within a few minutes, he'd claim the finishing touch to his day's uniform.

It was my turn now. My father pulled a small box from the corner of his suitcase, that was gaping open on the table. What could it be? He handed it to me.

"I couldn't resist this, Danny."

I took it eagerly. Oh my. The picture on the box showed a very realistic grey plastic camera and, beyond any wild expectation, the camera turned out to be a squirt gun. This would be a winner in the schoolyard and would take me right through until the end of the year!

"It needs to be put together, but I'll do it in the morning. Okay?"

"You bet, Daddy."

Late the next morning, my father was sitting at the kitchen table carefully putting together the camera-shaped squirt gun. I sat across from him. When my father finished, he got up, filled it with water, and gave it to me. Then he went to the bathroom. He often spent a long time in there, so I sat and waited patiently for him to return. After a while, I tried out the squirt gun. The trigger was designed as the button you pushed to take a picture. I pushed the button and heard the squishing sound of water. The water shot in an ellipse across the surface of the table. I was delighted. I was so happy my father was there and had been able to spend time putting it together for me. After conventions, he was often busy with his debit book or on the telephone with the office. I was anxious to show him the result of his handiwork.

The house was quiet. Marge was working, Beth was across the street, and my mother and the little kids were visiting down the street, likely paddling in our friend's tiny round swimming pool. I went through the dining room and turned toward the bathroom. What could be taking so long? I knocked on the bathroom door, first gently, then with more vigour. The quiet in the house was worrisome now. I ran outside and across the street to where Beth was sitting on the steps of our neighbour's porch.

"Daddy's in the bathroom," I said.

"So?"

"I knocked."

"So?"

"I knocked and knocked and he didn't answer."

Beth didn't say anything. She got up and walked briskly down the drive, across the street, and into our house. I watched, my mind frozen, without thinking, without speculating.

Beth appeared then, hurrying up our driveway, carrying the ladder. She went around the front of the house and disappeared down the other side. After a short while, Beth suddenly burst out of the front door of the house. She raced down the steps and turned up the street and ran like a wild animal toward our friend's house where my mother was visiting. For the first time, I felt the raspy cement through my thin cotton shorts.

Eddie's wife came out the front door.

"Hello, Daniel." She seemed surprised to see me. "Where'd your sister go?"

I didn't know how to answer.

"Daniel?"

"She went up the street."

"That's odd. She was going to help me sort clothes."

We saw my mother and sister racing down the street and disappear into the house. I had never seen my mother run before in my whole life and made no speculation about what might have triggered her unusual behaviour.

"Daniel, you stay here."

Mrs. Strang hurried down the drive, across the street, and into our house. I sat as told, my mind frozen, my heart beginning to race, as it had never done before.

My grandmother came out of the house and hurried over to me. She was a kindly, matronly woman with wire-rimmed glasses and papery skin that rolled into waves of wrinkles. She was usually calm, but now her eyes revealed great strain.

"Come inside."

She came up the steps and grasped my shoulder. She shepherded me into the Strang's house.

"Lie down, dear." She pointed to the couch. Just beyond the couch were baskets of laundry. I had never seen laundry baskets in a living room before. I sat on the couch.

"Lie down."

I lay down on the couch then. She held her hand against her cheek in a kind of anguish I had never seen before.

"Chappy's dead."

The two words did not belong together. My grandmother must have realized that.

"Your father's dead."

The door slammed open. Beth rushed in, screaming and crying at the same time. My grandmother hurried to her, took her by the arm, eased her up the stairs and they disappeared.

I looked up at the ceiling. There was a crack that broke into a scattered tangle, almost like a spider's web. My sister was on the other side of the crack, screaming incomprehensible words. The door slammed open again. Marge burst in, looked at me, then rushed upstairs. In a few moments there were two sets of wailing voices. "Daddy, Daddy, Daddy."

I tried to breathe, to somehow slow my beating heart.

When the door opened again, Father Thom came into the room. He was a very big man with a shock of black curly hair, wearing a black cassock and crisp Roman collar. He saw me lying on the couch then listened for a moment to the moaning and crying above him. He came to the couch and sat down on the edge.

"You know your father's dead, Danny?"

I looked away from his serene face and saw dust on the windowsill.

"I know it's hard, but I want you to try to be strong."

I didn't quite know what that meant, but like many things I heard from the pulpit, I expected that, at some point, the words would make sense.

"Your mother's going to need you."

Another riddle from the pulpit.

"I'm going to your sisters now."

He turned and walked heavily across the living room and started upstairs. After a short while, there was quiet behind the crack in the ceiling.

I could only think of one thing and said it to the empty room. "I didn't say goodbye."

∼

On the afternoon before the viewing at the funeral home, our house was filled with men and women, dressed in dark suits and equally dark dresses. There were grandparents, uncles and aunts, cousins from faraway, friends of the family, my father's colleagues, and many of our neighbours. There had never been so many people assembled before on our property. They were talking in hushed tones, gathered in clutches in the living room and dining room, on the porch, and on the front lawn.

The house was also overflowing with food. There were large platters of thinly sliced ham, bowls of potato salad and green salad, baskets of pretzels and potato chips on every flat surface. It was a spread far more lavish than Christmas or Easter. I weaved and wandered through the people, keeping my head down to try to avoid the possibility of conversation with anyone, including my sisters and brothers. Conversation seemed a particular danger, ever since Father Thom told me, "Your mother's going to need you." There seemed to be a whole lot of rituals, responsibilities, and sayings for the oldest son in the family. I was the oldest son, but I was only eleven.

I was conscious about what I wore. I loved my pants, white wool with specks of purple, highlighted by deep purple stitching down the outside seams. They were like pants my father would wear for semi-formal occasions like the celebration of a birthday or anniversary. I was wearing a white shirt, but the shirt had only small white buttons on the cuffs, rather than piercings for ornate cufflinks. I always admired the cufflinks on the chest of drawers in my parents' bedroom. My father had a fine collection and also a few decorative rings that he might wear on his right hand on special occasions. My shoes were a particular embarrassment. They were beige bucks, in vogue that season because of some movie star, but beige bucks were not black wing tips. Furthermore, I had no tie. The real shame, however, was that I didn't have a suit, not even a blazer or sports jacket. How could I be the one my mother would need without a suit on my back? How could I possibly stand in the doorway of the Family Room in the funeral home without a suit?

My father had been a sentinel in the doorway of that room for the visitations of his father, mother, and brother-in-law. He was always impeccably dressed in a sharp blue suit, a crisp white shirt, cufflinks, a subtle tie, and shiny wingtip shoes. He had a way of emanating calm to my mother and the other adults, but also, in a very special way, to the children. With him there, we were able to really relax in that room and not trouble ourselves with what was going to happen in the adjacent room later. There was always a long table filled with food, but for the children the only food of any interest were the sugar cookies. They were sweet white swirls with icing circles in the centre, delightful pale greens, yellows, and, the most sought-after, reds. I would take one at a time and return to the cozy couch and, in the sensuous way only a child knows, slip the cookie onto my tongue and wait with rising pleasure as the sugar melted in my mouth, followed by the bright sweetness of the icing. I would scamper for another and another. I would also glance from time to time toward the doorway to see the ever-calm presence of my father, shining somehow into the room, almost like a vision.

As some of the guests began glancing at their watches, I abandoned my invisibility to tell my mother in a calm and quiet way that I was going to walk over to the funeral home and meet the family there. My poor mother simply nodded to give permission. Once more invisible, I wove through the house, the porch, across the lawn, and slipped away. I thought it might look inappropriate if I took one of the two shortcuts to the funeral home, so I walked down the street. I slowly passed the eight brick homes on our side, gaining some of the calm that came from focusing on the shades and textures of the bricks. It was early afternoon; dusk and darkness were hours away. I studied the black iron streetlight standards with great care. At the end of our street, I slipped across to the other side so I could slowly pass the large house occupying the entire corner. I never knew who lived in that house. The distinguishing feature, aside from its sheer size, were the awnings over the windows. They were a posh touch, unusual for our neighbourhood. There was also a garage and always very nice dark cars parked in the driveway. I imagined the people to be of some mysterious origin, with a fascinating, maybe even illegal, occupation, clearly the result of my ever-active imagination.

I felt a surge of anxiety when I saw cars from my house beginning to move down the street then turn left toward the funeral home. I slowed my pace and stopped in front of the only large vacant lot in the neighbourhood. The lot had been excavated at least twice, as if preparing to build something, but all that remained at this point were a couple of large mounds of earth and rock. The lot had become a playground, suited to army games played by boys my age. The mounds were there to be scaled, then defended—like the flag-planting photo portrayed on Iwo Jima.

I reached the end of the vacant lot and saw the funeral home looming just ahead. In church, death was always the black of the vestments, but in the neighbourhood, death was the pristine white of the funeral home, which shone in the sun. I reached the walkway and turned in to take the long walk to the building. I decided to avoid the front entrance because the viewing room was just to the left of the door. I chose the side entrance instead. The parking lot behind the building was beginning to fill up. I walked up the two steps onto the small porch and opened the door. The smell of flowers was confusing, even sickening. I was no expert on flowers and came from a family that was indifferent to all but the two pots of geraniums that sat on ledges on either side of the porch. However, I knew by then that I really only enjoyed the scent of roses, not the tumult of scents of this funeral home. I moved into the hallway and stood before the podium with the guest book, lit by an elegant gold-stemmed lamp. There were only a few names at this point. I had written in the book when my grandparents were laid out, but I couldn't bring myself to do such a thing for my father. Instead, I went down the hall and slipped into the Family Room. I was relieved to see the long table already filled with food, including my beloved sugar cookies.

"I should have a suit," I whispered to myself.

∼

A SHORT WHILE LATER, I stood in front of the coffin with my mother by my side. I felt the presence of dozens of men and women behind me, and imagined my brothers and sisters still in the Family Room. My mother was brittle, shaking, cold. I had noticed in the miserably intense days since my father died that my mother did not like to be touched. She kept her distance from relatives and friends and, although caring and thoughtful with her children, including me, she did not hug, embrace, or, for that matter, even casually touch any of us.

I looked down at the kneeler in front of the coffin. I was certain we were expected to kneel there, much closer to the plush, satin-lined coffin. I risked a glance. It was not my father in that cold container. No, this was a wax image of someone like him. A wax image that was so very wrong. A kind of calm was frozen on its face I had never seen on my father's. A rosary was wrapped into its hands. My father never prayed the rosary. In fact, I had never seen him with one. My father would have a baseball glove in his hands or even a bottle of beer. But a rosary? Never.

I saw the funeral director out of the corner of my eye, moving into place at the foot of the coffin. I looked up and saw a wall of flowers, emblazoned with ribbons printed with words of the words, *Chappy* and *Love*. The scent of the flowers was sweet and sickly. I longed for the simple, pure scent of roses.

I felt a stirring behind me. I felt the visceral presence of the men most of all, realizing that each of them had a very clear notion about the rituals and responsibilities that the oldest son of the father who had died should be poised to perform.

I was clear about just one thing.

I would not touch that wax!

I felt my mother begin to sway slightly as she brought the tightly held hankie up to her trembling lips. I was sure now that something was about to happen. But what? The funeral director stepped forward and began to speak. He seemed to be speaking about my father. "A good man who loved his wife, his children, relatives, and friends, who was taken from us to the glory of heaven. And soon we will close the coffin and begin our journey to church. It's time to pay your last respects."

There was sniffling behind me now.

My mother collapsed to her knees on the kneeler. I hesitated a moment, then knelt beside her.

"You were so good," she said to the wax. "So good to the kids. So good to me."

The words wobbled from her trembling lips. She reached over the edge of the coffin and put her hand on the hands in the coffin. She stretched forward, rose up over the edge of the coffin, and leaned in to kiss those lips. She rested her head on the chest and sobbed.

I heard women crying behind me. I heard no sounds of men crying. I was clear and strong about not crying myself. Of all the things that had been said over the last few days, the strongest was that men don't cry. Of course, I knew from the hospital that big boys don't cry. This was different. The duty of the man of the family was not to cry. That was for women, girls, and little ones. I held on to that thought with a strength I didn't know I had. Along with the crying, there was movement. I heard the whimpering of my brothers and sisters, as they emerged from the Family Room. My mother was still resting on the wax's chest. I suddenly had a simple, sure idea.

"The others want to pass, Mom."

She heard me say that and moved slightly, but not with any purpose.

"We should let them."

She moved decisively then. She raised her head from its chest, patted the hands one last time, and then, with my hand softly on her elbow, stood up. We eased away and joined the funeral director at the foot of the coffin. My mother watched closely as the dozens of people passed by, genuflected, and made the Sign of the Cross. In some cases, they kneeled on the kneeler and bowed their heads in a longer prayerful moment.

My brothers and sisters came then. My two older sisters were serene with great sadness in their eyes, but calmness in their manner. The little ones were fidgety, confused by the press of people in the room, barely aware of the coffin. My heart began to break at the sight of the little ones, who unlike me and my older sisters, hadn't had the chance to feel the fullness of the love of our father and his hope for our futures.

Later that night, I tossed and turned in my bed, obsessed with thoughts about the men in my life. I often compared my father with the other men in the family. He was always dark to their pale, funny to their serious, happy to their sad, glamorous to their plain. It was all I could do not to cry. But I didn't.

~

In the morning, I stood with my mother at the back of our small church. The closed coffin was in front of us, a shining silver glow enhanced by the sun pushing through the stained-glass windows. There were dozens of people lined up behind us. At the end of the long central aisle, just on this side of the communion rail, was Father Thom and three altar boys, one with a golden cross, one with a swinging censer, and one with a silver container of holy water.

I remembered the Latin: *Et introibo ad altare Dei.* And I will go to the altar of God.

As I looked down the long aisle to Father Thom and the three altar boys, I suddenly realized that, unlike those behind me in the entrance and spilling out onto the front steps, I knew exactly what was going to happen through the entire ritual, including blessing the coffin with water and incense, the pace of the procession to the front of the church, the music the choir would be chanting, the way the priest would enter the sanctuary, and every single response to every single incantation or prayer the priest would recite. All in exquisite detail.

I found strength. The muscles in my legs and arms relaxed. My voice gained depth. I felt whole, calm and strong, the way I imagined my father must have felt as the sentinel in the door of the Family Room.

The rituals ticked away like a finely made watch. I moved with a calm coolness through the Mass, through the ride to the cemetery, through the prayers over the freshly dug grave with the piles of wilting flowers, through the return in the long black limousine, even through the breakfast at our house the next morning. My uncle made the breakfast and it was like my grandmother would make, with fluffy scrambled eggs, perfectly fried slices of ham, nicely browned toast.

But, to my confusion as I helped bring things to the dining-room table, my uncle said the large glass pitcher of juice needed ice cubes added to it. My father never drank his juice with ice cubes.

And, after that morning, I never did either.

Passion

Passion

Thomas Aquinas Seminary sat majestically at the top of a rise, looking down on the run of the mighty river. My mother turned into the long driveway and started towards the massive new structure. The brochure said that the new building was fashioned of cream stone quarried from the southern hills with a design borrowed from the seminaries of Europe, featuring a central chapel and adjacent wings. The long lawn leading up from the highway was gardened tenderly. Clusters of bushes and plants caressed a circular walking path. And, along the way, statues of saints with stone benches for meditation.

"It's so...saintly."

"Saintly?" I asked.

"You know what I mean."

I said nothing because, as sometimes happened, I had no idea what my mother meant. I looked at the ornate building and, instead of saintly, I saw powerful, which led me to a question. What did that power mean?

I didn't think of that question in the months leading up to the decision to enter the seminary. I spent every morning, through the glorious spring and summer of 1963, in the more modest confines of St. Margaret's Church. The cozy church was spare and simple, with small, intimate spaces for the side altars. I would pull open the wooden side door of the stucco church, enter the nave, and slip into a pew near the side altar devoted to the Blessed Virgin Mary. The spot also afforded me a perfect vista of the door opposite the altar, where, shortly after my arrival, a large family would enter. I would look up at the lovely face of the statue of Mary and then down at the equally lovely face of Ginny Martin. She was one grade behind me, and like the other girls her age, was quickly becoming a woman with fully defined curves in all the right places. The curves would go away only when I took the rosary out of my pocket and begin a frantic recitation of Hail Mary's, trying to keep my imagination on the appropriate religious mysteries, not the mysteriousness of the lovely girl on the other side of church.

This struggle seemed to define my life in the summer of 1963 more than anything. I spent that season without a steady job, instead going to the country club to caddy for the doctors, lawyers, and entrepreneurs who lived in the fine homes in the hills around the golf course. Like the older boys on the baseball field, who had adopted me and drawn me into their select circle, the young man who chose the caddies and matched them with golfers favoured me. I always managed to heave the heavy bags of the medical specialists or corporate lawyers who, after eighteen holes of relatively mediocre golf, would dig into their thick wallets and pull out a nice set of dollar bills. Stuffing those singles into the pocket of my Levi's I'd head for the swimming pool and, hopefully, a late afternoon of admiring Ginny Martin from afar.

I usually hitchhiked home first, pulled my swim suit from the line in the dark basement, grabbed a towel from the pile on the table next to the aging washer, and hurried through the intricate path of short cuts through yards and parking lots until I reached the entrance to the pool. The woman who owned the pool had an electric wheel chair. With her gnarled hand on the power stick, she would drive her chair from her nearby house to a spot at the end of the lunch counter on the balustrade overlooking the pool. She had a microphone for announcements and books and ledgers to keep track of the business. She hired a brother and sister from the neighbourhood to operate the admission desk and lunch counter.

One day I showed my season's pass at the admission desk and quickly slipped through the entry and down the ramp to the boys' change room. The space was musty and damp, filled with the echoing banter of boys made hyper by the exhilaration of swimming. I quickly undressed, stuffed my clothes into a locker, and pulled on my swim trunks before making my way through the door to the pool. The shock of sudden bright sun never ceased to thrill me. Feeling salty sweat on my shoulders, I quickly ran to the edge of the shining blue water and dove, staying underwater for as long as my breath would last, and eventually made it to the other side of the pool. I slid easily out of the water and hurried to the basketball court next to the pool. A gaggle of boys were shooting and, when I arrived, they quickly became two teams of three and a game began.

I had more than hoops on my mind, however. Ginny Martin was on the grass beyond the basketball court, with her gang of girlfriends, soaking up the sun in their multi-coloured two-piece suits. Ginny wore a mocha brown suit and her pale décolleté flashed as brightly as the sun when she stood to shake out her towel. The sudden flash stole my attention, causing me to lose the ball and give up an easy shot to my opponent. I continued with those quick glances, risking further shame on the court, but never in a million years would I even consider going onto the grass and approaching the girls and opening a conversation with the object of my desire.

And in the holy confines of St. Margaret's Church, morning after morning, when I should have had nothing more on my mind than the decision to go to the seminary, I found that mind filled with images of perfect white roundness encased in mocha brown.

The first flash of the decision to become a priest shot through me when I was eleven, standing in front of my father's casket at his funeral Mass. The press of men behind me, uncles and neighbours, had swarmed as soon he died, buzzing with plans for what I should do with my life. I suddenly realized that being a priest would be a sure way to avoid those plans. I began to head in that direction in high school and, in my final year, thought a visit to the monastery would be useful.

I visited the ancient enclave with two friends, brainy football players like me. The monastery was deep in the southern hills and the buildings seemed to emerge from the Middle Ages as if by magic. We were each assigned cots in the spare dormitory, then led to the balcony of the chapel, overlooking a sea of monks in heavy brown robes. They chanted hymns at the appointed hours in the canonical cycle, descending on the chapel from their cubicles during the night and from the fields or the brewery during the day. The brewery was said to make one of the truly fine beers, using a recipe from deep in the Middle Ages.

I leaned forward on the kneeler to get a better look at the monks, and then, rising like incense in the air, Gregorian chant filled every space in the holy place. I felt an impossible peace at that moment, something never experienced before, but promised by the priests at retreats I'd attended over the last two years. They promised serenity sanctioned by the divine presence of the Holy Trinity: Father, Son, and Holy Ghost. I was prone to spells of imaginative wandering and in some of those spells felt that kind of serenity and came to believe it was sent from Heaven above. In the chapel in the hills, Heaven swirling around me in song, I made up my mind. Or more precisely, my mind was magically made up. It didn't feel like logic or reason or, as my uncles and neighbours suggested, the outcome of a list of pros and cons; no, it was a spontaneous and complete yielding to something that I felt was far beyond me, but mine to embrace.

I tried to return to that moment whenever the sight of Ginny Martin seemed too great to bear. I reasoned, or more precisely imagined, that the swirl of sound would always waft me into a peaceful, holy place, where the flash of soft whiteness encased in loving brown would never intrude. And fortunately, as my mother pulled the car into a parking space in front of the chapel, an image of soft whiteness had no chance to slip in.

"Will you be all right, honey?"

"I will, Mom."

"You don't want me to come with you to meet the dean?"

"The papers said to just drop us off. I'm to take my suitcase to his office and wait for my interview and room assignment. It's all laid out in the papers."

"I know that, honey. But..."

"Mom, it's really okay."

"I'll write you."

"I know you will."

"Give me a hug."

My mother wasn't really the hugging type. She had a personal reserve that seemed strange for a woman who had seven children, so this took me by surprise. I wasn't much of a hugger either. For that matter, it seemed to be alien to our whole family. My father was the hugger, the toucher, the laugher, the spark of life. But he'd been dead for six years. After we got out of the car, I approached her and put my arms around her and even pulled her towards me. I picked up the sweet scent of her lipstick as she leaned in to kiss me on the cheek. Then she pulled away, drew a hankie from her slacks, touched it to her tongue, and wiped away the red.

"We can't have the dean see lipstick on your cheek."

"Bye, Mom."

"Christmas will be here soon, honey."

I turned to look at the striking green lawn rolling down to the road. Soon?

"Okay, Mom. I better go."

She seemed on the verge of tears.

I quickly picked up my suitcase and turned towards the chapel. I hurried to the massive stone steps and climbed to the heavy wooden doors, then looked back to see the car turn on to the highway. I grabbed the brass door handle, tugged the door open, and entered Thomas Aquinas Seminary. The entryway opened on the huge chapel with the green marble floor, which caught the light from the stained glass windows. The rows of shining pews marched towards a majestic trio of white marble altars. This chapel, with its brilliant opulence, was the way I pictured the Roman chapels described by the bright young priests who taught me in high school. And then I slowly turned left and trudged down the long hallway to a frosted glass office door, which bore the words *Dean of Admissions* in stark black letters. I dropped my suitcase beside two others outside the door and opened it.

There was one other boy in the waiting room. He looked up as I sidled towards the vacant chair but didn't say a word. He was dressed in a collegiate, sophisticated way, with sharply creased slacks, a button-down oxford shirt, a sports coat, and penny loafers. I was wearing black Levis, a casual shirt, and low-cut black gym shoes. The papers advised dressing casually. It slowly dawned on me that the word did not mean the same for everyone.

The door to the inner office opened and another well-dressed boy came out. The priest who followed him was short, greying, and fidgety, wearing a black cassock and white Roman collar.

"Ah," he said, looking directly at me. "And you might be?"

"Dan James," I said.

"Indeed! From St. Margaret's. In the western hills."

"That's right, Father."

"We'll see you after Mr. Kehoe from St. John's. In the eastern hills."

I smiled. The boy left the waiting room and Mr. Kehoe followed the priest into his office. While they were inside, no one else arrived. I had some idea from the papers of what the priest might say, but with my misunderstanding of the word to describe how to dress, I began to fear that I might have misunderstood everything else. When the Dean and Mr. Kehoe came back into the waiting room, I quickly stood.

"Come, come, Mr. James."

We went into the office. The dean settled himself behind his large desk, scattered with files and piles of paper. Behind him the tall windows revealed a striking inner courtyard with the same careful landscaping as the rolling front lawn. A paved pathway circled through the landscaping, likely where the priests/professors paced while reciting their daily prayers. And along the pathway, alcoves with statues of saints.

"Mr. James, I am Dean D'Amico, but it will suffice to call me Father."

"Yes, Father."

On the wall to the priest's left was a large framed El Greco reproduction, depicting Jesus with a crown of thorns, bearing a massive cross, his eyes fixed on the heavens. The priest noticed my glance.

"Do you have a devotion to the Passion?"

I wasn't sure what that meant and quickly decided not to take a chance.

"Ah...no, Father."

"The Passion is a most marvelous mystery, holding countless themes for prayer and meditation. It became my devotion many years ago when I was a boy entering the seminary, just like you."

"I see, Father." Not really. Devotion to the Passion? It seemed like some kind of sacred riddle.

"Most marvelous mystery."

"Yes, Father."

The dean proceeded through a fairly mundane set of questions about my high school courses and grades. He seemed annoyed that my grades weren't consistently excellent and wasn't interested in my wide range of extra-curricular activities, everything from football to drama to the school newspaper. He also seemed to be searching for something that might send me soaring as a seminarian. I began to wonder about that. What would this new life, inside the walls of the seminary, hold for me?

"You'll be rooming with a boy from Pittsburgh in 214."

"Thank you, Father."

I left the office and picked up my suitcase. The staircase at the end of the hallway had a railing fashioned from exquisite walnut and twisted wrought iron. After reaching the top of the stairs I went down the hall until I reached 214. I opened the door. A tall, lanky boy was plopped on one of the two beds reading a paperback. There was already a long line of paperbacks on the shelves above the desk next to his bed. I didn't have a single book in my big brown suitcase. I set it down. The boy didn't take his eyes off his book. I approached the bed.

"Hey. My name's Dan James."

He kept his eyes on the book.

"I'm your roommate."

The eyes glanced over the top of the book.

"I figured that, James."

The eyes slipped back down again.

"What's yours?"

"What's my what?"

"Your name?"

"Didn't the little Italian tell you?"

The little Italian?

"Deano."

"Dean D'Amico?"

"He's the only Deano down there."

"No, he didn't mention your name. Only that you're from Pittsburgh. You a Pirate fan?"

"A what?"

"You know, the baseball team."

I noticed the title of the book now. *Down and Out in London and Paris.*

"I don't do baseball. I do books."

"I see."

I figured this conversation wasn't going to go any further at the moment, especially since he'd turned towards the wall to continue reading. I saw that the book had been written by George Orwell and even remembered that he'd also written *1984*, a book we read in high school. I hauled my suitcase over to the unclaimed bed. There was a desk facing the wall; it looked out on the inner courtyard through tall windows, like the ones in the dean's office. A chest of drawers sat on the other side of the bed and next to it a sink and medicine cabinet. The other side of the room was a mirror image of my side. There were also small closets with sliding doors on either side of the door. I loaded my things into the chest of drawers, the medicine cabinet, and the closet. That didn't take long. I walked to my desk, slid the chair around to face my roommate's bed, and sat down.

"I didn't get your name."

The boy continued to face the wall with the book close to his nose.

"I got yours, James."

Finally, he dropped the book and turned over, slipping his hands behind his head, looking at the ceiling.

"And yours?"

"Gabe," he said.

"From Gabriel? The archangel?"

"The very same."

"And your last name?"

"By that I assume you mean, my surname."

"Surname?"

"Just what kind of high school did you go to, James?"

I usually had a pretty good grip on my temper with strangers.

"Why don't we call time out on this."

"Time out?"

I relished this, confusing him with a word rather than a punch.

"From the ping pong."

"Ping pong?"

My pleasure increased immensely.

"The back and forth bullshit. This is a small room. We're the only two here. That kind of thing."

"Oh, I see. That kind of thing."

"Great. Now, where were we? Oh, yes. Your…surname."

"Right. Sullivan. Gabriel Sullivan. First and only son of John L. and Mary G. Sullivan of Pittsburgh, Pennsylvania. Home of United States Steel."

"And the Pirates."

"As you suggest, the Pirates."

"Did they name your father after the boxer?"

"Well, there you go. The first person I ever met who knew that."

"How's this then? John *Lawrence* Sullivan."

"Well, I'll be."

"I'm likely the only person in Ohio who knows that."

"And Pennsylvania, too!"

He smiled to himself and took his hands from behind his head. I knew that I had managed to break into him for the first time. Again, I was tickled that it was with words, not fists.

"I went to Weller," I said.

He looked a bit confused.

"Weller High School. We name our schools after dead archbishops."

"I went to Ignatius Loyola."

"I see. You do dead saints. He was founder of the Jesuits. Right?"

"Well there. You do seem to know some stuff."

"Yea," I said. "I pay attention to some…stuff, but not others."

"Like?"

"Trigonometry, physics. That kind of thing."

"We got that in common. It seems to come to me, but I hate it."

"What do you like?

He held the book up. "Left-wing populism, at the moment. I resisted for years, but my father eventually got me going."

"What does he do?"

"He's an organizer for the United Steel Workers."

I had never known anyone who worked for a union.

"My father was an insurance salesman."

"Was?"

"He died six years ago."

"I see. Hey, do you want to do a few loops around the courtyard?"

"Loops?"

"That's what they call walks around the pathway."

"Sure. Why not?"

We left the room in a spirit of connection and wound through the building to the courtyard entrance. There were a few seminarians doing exactly what we were about to do, going round and round on the pathway, in pairs or small groups, with explosions of talk, talk, talk. Gabe began talking as soon as his feet touched the path. He continued on about his father and his work with the union. Men would come to their home on the north side, near the confluence of the two small rivers that formed the mighty Ohio. There were cigars and shouts late into the night as the men squabbled about strategy, tactics, and timing. I had never heard these kinds of things before. In the white-collar world of my father, his colleagues dressed and talked like late-night television hosts. As we made loop after loop with the dozens of young men who like us seemed to be getting to know one another, I entered a world that I had no idea even existed. I had become somewhat interested in politics since the election of John Kennedy in 1960. I had even watched the Democratic Convention that finally chose him as the candidate. And I was over-joyed that he had become the first Catholic President of the United States. But unions and boycotts and strikes, all of that was way beyond my ken.

We stopped after a while at one of the alcoves and sat on the stone bench in front of the statue of Saint Thomas Aquinas. He looked down on us sternly. I remembered then: Aquinas was the logician.

"What about you, James?"

"What about what?"

"What sets you on fire? What's your passion?"

This brought back the conversation in the dean's office. He was talking about his devotion to the passion of Christ. Gabe was talking about something else. His words drove me into myself, like the time in the chapel in the hills of Kentucky.

"I don't know," I said. I felt that was one of the bravest things that had ever come from my mouth.

"Well, it's time to find out."

"You may be right."

We got up, took another loop in silence, and then headed back into the dormitory.

∼

THE MARCH TOWARDS CHRISTMAS WAS studded with an incredibly heavy load of courses, without a single soft spot. Latin, logic, theology, literature, history, biology, mathematics. The dean told us to organize our days into fifteen-minute units, so we could plow through all of the assigned work and still have lights out by 9:00 pm. Gabe ignored the urging and carried on much as he had that first day, reading books from his shelf, stacking the text books on the floor under the desk, yet somehow absorbing the essence of every single lecture and delivering easily on the tests and assignments. I was overwhelmed as I had never been. I began to treasure the long times spent in chapel for Mass, meditation, and rosary, when I could slip away from the whole situation, enter the mystery of my own dreamy world, dabble with images from the pool in the summer, create flash-fast tales of life outside the walls of the seminary. And, from time to time, think about that word, *passion*.

The loops with Gabe continued. He was a great raconteur when he picked up a head of steam on a topic, and his choice of topics seemed endless. He skipped from technology to theology, rock and roll to rhythm and blues, politics to revolution. He became most intense, however, on the topic of civil rights and the dynamic leader Martin Luther King Jr. Our preferred spot was under the stern glare of Thomas Aquinas the Logician after endless loops. Gabe got to civil rights one morning after breakfast in the refectory. We always ate in silence listening to readings from the *Lives of the Saints*.

Gabe screwed his face with intensity that morning.

"My father and his buddies are…racists."

I had begun to hear that word on television without having a real clear understanding of what it was or how it operated. I had a long-standing connection with Cassie, the black woman who had come to our home to iron my father's shirts. Even though my father had been dead for six years, my mother still made visits to Cassie's home in the basin, the centre of the black community. I came with her a few times and always felt comfortable with the people and the neighbourhood.

"Negroes are trying to get into unions in Pittsburgh," said Gabe. "You don't hear much about it on television, but it drives my father right up the wall."

"Why'd you get interested?"

"The more he railed against them, the more I wanted to support them. I began to read a lot and found Martin Luther King's sermons and, when my father wasn't around, I devoured them. And then King went to Washington."

I remembered coming home from caddying at the country club one afternoon in August and watching on television as a mass of people listened to Dr. King's rolling, rhythmic words. "I have a dream," he said, over and over, and it sounded like poetry from the pulpit, magically stirring the crowd. I was surprised that my grandfather was watching with intense interest. He was a kind and generous man, but he had never shown much interest in politics or social issues.

"What did your dad make of it?" I asked Gabe.

"When he found the sermons in my room, he wasn't amused. But he taught me to be my own person and, by God, I'm going to be my own person."

"I never had to deal with that."

"It's the old Oedipal thing."

"The what?"

"Here we go again. Another deficit in your education."

"All right, Gabe. Let's not go there, okay?"

We were becoming close through these loops and talks and, for me, with four sisters and two baby brothers, it felt a bit like having a big brother. I guess brothers get sharp at times. But I did enjoy being a learner under the gaze of Aquinas.

"It's a Greek myth taken up by Jungians."

"This isn't helping me."

Gabe went on to give me a mini-lecture on the Oedipal complex, complete with lengthy trips through the winding paths of Greek mythology and contemporary psychiatry. I didn't know what he was talking about. But I did know that it was about standing up to his father on an important matter like race. And on loop after loop, he told me the tale of the civil rights movement and the role of Dr. King.

The loops became the only part of the seminary that gave me joy. Although the professors were brilliant and beautifully educated, each had his own unique and challenging style. The material was dense and complicated. I'd managed to keep up with things in high school by learning to pay attention when the teacher seemed to be putting exclamation points on things. Somehow I would pull these things from memory on the inevitable tests. But this was different. The intricacies of Latin plunged into the labyrinth of logic, twisted through the ripples of literature, and disappeared into the black hole of theology. I spent most of my days exhausted, waiting for the times after breakfast, lunch, and dinner when I was able to do loops with Gabe, wandering through whatever he happened to be reading or thinking about at the moment.

I also treasured the times in chapel, wandering around in my dreamy musings, paying just enough attention to the Mass or meditation or rosary to avoid missing any of the required responses. I would often stare at one of the older seminarians kneeling at the side altar dedicated to St. Joseph. He held his arms outstretched, his body forming the shape of a cross. He did this for hours at a time, the kind of self-abnegation hinted at in *Lives of the Saints*. I couldn't seem to retrieve the magic of the moment in the monastery when becoming a priest seemed to be the most certain future for me. I certainly could never match the simple, humble devotion of so many of the seminarians. Did I really belong?

Things took a dramatic turn in the middle of October with the rector's retreat. Monsignor Richter was a stentorian figure in his sixties with a forceful voice and round cheeks framing sharp blue eyes behind wire-rim glasses. He led his annual retreat from the high perch of the pulpit to the left of the main altar. He peppered the opening with references to the purging wonders of the sacrament of confession and then began to parse the Act of Contrition.

"Oh, my God, I am heartily sorry for having offended Thee," he intoned. He had the sea of seminarians in the tight grip of his fierce face and commanding voice as he imagined for us how God must feel violated by every single sin we ever committed or even thought about committing, reminding us that sins didn't require action but could simply be thought about or imagined and still smack God squarely in the face. And of course, the only possible response was to become a supplicant before Him by expressing the depth of our sorrow. He went on.

"I detest all of my sins because of Thy just punishment, but most of all because they offend Thee, my God, who art all-good and deserving of all my love."

The rector roared through this like a raging lion, moving from our sins to the inevitable punishment, and then to the deep tragedy of offending the goodness of the God of Love. I squirmed through his exegesis, along with the seminarians all around me, feeling the need to take a look down a dark corridor to the blackness that seemed to cover my soul.

"I firmly resolve, with the help of Thy grace, to sin no more and to avoid the near occasion of sin. Amen."

The fire from the pulpit was turned down to a flicker, with an emphasis on the resolve required to stop sinning and to keep away from anything close to a sin in the making. At this point, with the brilliant October light streaming through the stained-glass windows, I realized that I was in very deep trouble. And the name of that trouble was Ginny Martin.

She hadn't left me when I opened door to the seminary a month and a half ago; no, she haunted most nights as I tossed from one side of the bed to the other in the intense quiet of the dormitory. I had experienced a similar kind of quiet in the hills of Kentucky, but that quiet had been filled with sonorous Gregorian chant. On these sleepless nights, however, she came to me, not as she did in the nave of the church; no, instead as she did on the grass at the swimming pool, with the soft brown of her two-piece bathing suit, revealing the brilliance of her round and lovely breasts. And on one recent night in the dormitory, a swelling emerged in the centre of me and quickly turned into a length of hardness, which my hand turned into an eruption of spurts, impossible to control, soaking my pajamas with a sticky wetness.

This agitated memory caused me severe discomfort as I kept my eyes on the imposing jowl of Monsignor Richter. At that point, he began to take the sea of seminarians through an examination of conscience. I felt a great sense of relief as he plowed through the first five of the Ten Commandments, realizing I didn't have a single sin to take behind the heavy curtain of the confessional. However, when he reached the sixth commandment, my anxiety rose with sudden fierceness. He went through three specific things to examine.

"Have you kept away from the near occasion of sin?"

I felt a tingling at the back of my neck.

"Have you deliberately taken pleasure in impure thoughts?"

I felt goose bumps shooting down my spine.

"Have you committed any wilful impure actions?"

I felt a sudden sweat break on my wide forehead.

I didn't even hear the words of the rest of the examination of conscience. I knew already that, to avoid abstaining from Holy Communion, likely the only seminarian to do so, I would have to go into that confessional this very day. A dread far greater than any, ever.

The rector announced that priests would be entering the confessionals in chapel within minutes, so confession would be available to all who wished to go. I certainly didn't wish to go, but there was simply no choice. The rector advised that he would lead us through the prayer before confession. I heard the whole sea of seminarians kneel before my own body would respond; then fell to the kneeler. He began in a resonant, echoing voice:

"Look upon me, Lord Jesus, most wretched of all sinners; have pity on me, and give me the light to know my sins, true sorrow for them, and a firm purpose of never committing them again."

The chapel was suddenly still. And then I could hear soft footfalls on the marble floor. I saw one of my professors enter the confessional closest to my pew and realized that, on top of everything, I would have to confess to someone who might have a chance of recognizing me through the translucent screen separating priest from penitent. I didn't have a moment to ponder this brutal fact before seminarians began leaving my pew to stand in line at the confessional. I was third in line. I weirdly hoped that the two boys ahead of me were notorious sinners with lots to share in the dim light of the confessional. That wasn't the case. They spent only enough time for a venial sin or two. I approached the ornate wooden enclave, drew back the heavy velvet curtain, and entered. I knelt down. The space was dark as night for a mere moment, then the screen's cover slid open, and there, was the serious and solemn profile of my history professor. Father Berkeley was a scholar trained at the Sorbonne in Paris; he had an encyclopedic knowledge of the French Revolution and a glinting smile when it came to describing the design and effectiveness of a guillotine.

"Yes, my son." he intoned.

I took a deep yet unsatisfying breath.

"Bless me, Father, for I have sinned," I began. "My last confession was two weeks ago."

I stopped, even though I had never stopped at that point before.

"And..."

"And these are my...sins."

I stopped again, this time literally gasping for air.

"Yes, my son..."

"I had…impure thoughts."

"What was the nature of these thoughts?"

I did not expect that question. This hadn't been in the examination of conscience. I had never confessed that sin before, so had nothing prepared.

"The nature, my son…"

I suddenly began to doubt that what I imagined that night was an "impure thought." I was momentarily tongue-tied.

"There are others waiting," he said.

"I thought about a girl."

"What girl? A family member?"

"No, Father."

"A friend?"

I was beginning to think like a lawyer, not an altar boy.

"No, Father."

"Then who?" There was irritation in those two words.

"A girl in my school."

"And exactly what was the 'thought' about the girl in your school?"

Even a lawyer couldn't squirm out of this.

"I thought I wanted to…touch her."

"I see," he said. "Where did you want to touch her?"

Lawyer again: at the swimming pool. No, that wouldn't work.

"On her breasts."

"I see. This was an impure thought. Any other impure thoughts to confess?"

"No, Father."

"Any other sins?"

"Yes, Father. I did a willful impure action."

"With the girl in your school?"

"No, Father." The priests at my parish were never this persistent.

"Who was she?"

"It wasn't a 'she', Father."

"You did an impure action with another boy?"

"No, Father."

I suddenly realized that the seminarians in line behind me must be speculating that I was the biggest sinner in the universe, with so much time ticking away.

"Explain, my son."

"I did an impure action with…myself."

"Did you masturbate?"

I had never heard a priest say that word.

"I did, Father."

"When? This summer?"

I did not believe what I was hearing. I could commit another sin by lying, but that would only complicate and further blacken my soul.

"This week."

I heard a deep sigh. "In the seminary?"

"Yes, Father."

"Are there more sins to confess?"

"No, Father."

"Okay then. For your penance, I want you to pray an entire rosary and meditate on the sorrowful mysteries. And in so doing, gain the will to never commit that sin again."

"Yes, Father." I had to finish properly. "And for these and all the sins of my past life, I am heartily sorry." He said the Latin prayer required for the sacrament of confession and then made the solemn blessing with the sign of the cross.

"Go in peace, my son."

The screen slid shut, sending me into darkness again. I got up quickly and pulled back the curtain. The boys in line looked away from me, as if they were embarrassed. I slipped back into the pew, knelt down, and pulled my rosary from my pocket and began to recite the prayers. They seemed endless; the other seminarians prayed far lighter penances and left the chapel. I was left by myself after a while, a miserable wretch, racing through the prayers in a frantic rush to finish. And finally, I was done.

I left the chapel, slipped through the dormitory, and went into the courtyard looking for Gabe. I began to make fevered loops, my mind's eye stuck in the confines of the confessional. I paid no notice to the curling of the leaves on the bushes or the tinge of colour on the tall trees. I wound around to the front of the building. I started down the pathway on that part of the grounds. There were straggling pairs of seminarians on this path, but still no Gabe. I stopped for a moment and looked towards the driveway and the highway, which eventually led to my home in the western hills. I really wanted to run down that road and never come back again. But something was beginning in the back of my mind, and it had nothing to do with impure thoughts or actions; no, it had to do with the question that Gabe posed to me weeks ago.

"What's your passion?"

~

AS AUTUMN DEEPENED AND THE leaves turned a spectacular splash of yellow, orange, and red, I began to spend free time on Saturday nights with Gabe on the field behind the seminary. Gabe had picked up a hobby and I tagged along. He discovered that the seminary had a high-quality telescope and, having an ever-growing range of interests, decided that he needed to try his hand at astronomy. The library was helpful because at the end of a long line of books about Latin, logic, and theology there were four books on the rudiments of astronomy. Gabe set aside his populist books for a while and dove into astronomy with the fury of a true explorer. Before long he knew enough to find the perfect spot on the field to set up the telescope and explore the mystic wonder of the planets.

Gabe continued to remind me of the enormous gaps in my education, which included anything to do with the natural world. The blaze of stars and blinking of planets was one of these gaps.

The time we saw Saturn was the most magical. On a wonderfully fresh October night, under an arc of magnificent stars, Gabe carefully adjusted the telescope and its settings and finally announced in a celebratory tone: "The rings of ice!" He backed away from the eyepiece and led me forward, until my face touched the chilled silver casing.

And there, in a brightness that almost took my breath way, was the brilliant sight of a perfect ball, its shining rings turning endlessly in a display of celestial magic. "Oh, my God," I whispered. It seemed that anything more than a whisper would be a sacrilege.

We continued to spend those autumn nights on the football field with the telescope and soon I began to feel like science was something I could master, at least the kind of science I could see through the eyepiece of a telescope. Of course, there was endless talk about a whole universe of topics, but it was the exhilaration of being under the arc of an autumn sky, each one so different, that generated the most excitement. I was unable to turn that excitement into some kind of meditational theme, but to simply experience it made me realize how much wonder there was in the world to relish and treasure.

I can't say that was true of the courses, assignments and tests. But as November brought the snow and cold that stopped our astronomy evenings, I began to discover what might drive me. And curiously for one who had read no more than two or three serious books in his whole life, I found myself falling in love with a shelf of books in the library. I had become fond of one of my professors, by far the most eccentric, who had a knack of turning words on a page into rolling, rhythmic tones that held my attention like a powerful magnet. Father O'Reirdan, like my own father, had grown up in the basin before it became a black neighbourhood. He was also from a working class family and benefitted from the good education possible through the parochial school system. He entered the seminary as a young boy, excelled in academics and decided to specialize in literature. Like many other brilliant seminarians, he was sent overseas for graduate studies, and in his case, that meant Oxford University. Along the way at Oxford, the working class boy became a thoroughly cultured Englishman, with an accent and manner that would have been welcome in the exclusive clubs of London. He began the term with lectures on the various genres of literature, then settled into his own love - the modern novel.

He sent us to the library with a list from which we were to choose a novel to read and then write an analytic essay. I wandered down the aisles with the list in my hand and stopped in front of *Young Lonigan* by

James T. Farrell. I liked the look of the boy on the cover, as tough as I wanted to be. I ended up digging into it in much the same way as Gabe dug into his books. I was captured by the description of Chicago street life, drawn with verve and precision, and featuring wise-cracking characters my own age. After swallowing the book in frantic gulps, I returned to the library and found the next two books in the trilogy: *The Young Manhood of Studs Lonigan* and *Judgment Day*. I was hooked.

Just as Gabe had taken me on wanderings through civil rights, I began to take him on wanders through an imagined Chicago. It was exhilarating for me to find words to tell him about these things, and even more exhilarating to realize that I could also find words when I sat down to write the essay. I started to believe that this somehow might be the answer to the question Gabe had posed: "What's your passion?" The deal was sealed when my essay came back with an A+ on the top of the page and this message scrawled in the margin: "A fine explication with real depth of understanding, Mr. James. I believe you have the makings of a scholar. At least of street life…"

These words gave me the feeling that my passion might be a life of reading and writing, but what did that have to do with eight years of Latin, logic, and theology leading to a long lifetime as a priest? It gave me pause. And I began to try to review exactly how I had come to be where I was.

When I stood behind my father's coffin six years earlier, I knew as an experienced altar boy all there was to know about liturgical ceremonies. With a cold realization I suddenly understood that the men behind me, smothering me with advice about my life, had absolutely no idea what was about to happen in this ceremony, the Mass of the Dead. And I did. I had a surge of strength: I felt confidence and a sense of direction. It opened a path to a place where those men had never been. This led to the dreamy moment at the monastery in the hills of Kentucky when I chose the path to the seminary.

And here I was, swimming in Latin, logic, theology, with only the life jacket of literature to keep me from going under.

In a sudden break in the emergence of winter, the sun showered me and Gabe with warmth on a late Friday afternoon, as we settled on the bench under Aquinas's stony glare. I fumbled at first but quickly discovered my newfound ability to bring clarity to a jumble of notions battling in my head. And I began to recount the path of my decision-making about coming into the seminary and the implications of leaving. He listened respectfully and then took a deep breath.

"You're beginning to answer the question."

Of course, I knew what the question was.

"Yeah," I said.

"I thought you would, James."

"Really?"

"Yea. When we would argue on our loops, you made me think. I believed that nobody, including my father, made me think about anything. And you did. Because you had grit and guts."

The sun seemed to be shining more brightly now.

"When will you leave?"

"I'm not sure. I have to talk to the dean."

"Old Deano."

"Yeah, old Deano."

There was a commotion at the door to the dormitory and seminarians roared onto the path like a raging river. A seminarian from our floor hurried over to the alcove.

"What's up?" I asked

"They shot Kennedy! The president's dead!"

There was not a single thing to say.

"We're to go to chapel," he said. "Right now."

~

THE NEXT FOUR DAYS WERE an agony of praying in chapel and watching tragic images on television. A mass sorrow began to emerge, like in the Middle Ages after the death of a king, a numbing that shut down thought and opened up rivers of emotion. It swept away the lingering anger for those men who'd suffocated me with well-meaning advice after my father died. I cried, night after night. I suffered sorrow, over... what? The elegant Jackie? The sweet children? The mass of mourners lining the streets as the cortege made its way to the cemetery? My father's image mingled with the image of the young president, and my endless tears came for both of them at once.

The days of mourning wound down, leaving the whole of the seminary in a state of exhaustion. The classes had stopped, but the cycle of Mass, meditation, and rosary continued. Meditation time gave me the long moments I needed to prepare me for my inevitable meeting with the dean and my later conversations with my mother and grandfather. I was sure that the dean would be the most difficult, my mother the most understanding, and my grandfather the most heart-broken. But always there was Gabe with me, day after day, under the statue of Thomas Aquinas in the chilly, and now grey, last days of November.

"Are you sure, Danny?"

He sat on the stone bench, his long legs crossed, a fresh pile of books stuffed into his knapsack.

"I am."

"You got the answer?"

I looked across the courtyard to the window of the dean's office. I pointed.

"For him?"

"No, Dan. Not Deano. You. Your passion."

"I know that being here, studying to be a priest, isn't even close."

"Then what?"

"I want to be like you, Gabe."

He roared in sudden laughter. "Like me? You got to be kidding."

"I want to be a wild reader and...writer."

I looked up at the stern, stony face of Thomas Aquinas. "He's the logician, isn't he, Gabe?"

"You got it. This leads to that, leads to the other thing."

"Who's the mystic?"

"Augustine."

"Right! I kind of think you're like him. A guy who loves wild things like astronomy and civil rights. I want to be like that."

"I'll be!"

"No, Gabe. I'll be!"

Gabe suddenly thrust out his hand. I took it. He shook my hand with great vigour.

"You know what?"

"What, Gabe?"

"I'm going to miss you."

"You know what?

"What?"

"I'm going to remember you as long as I live."

"Well, there you go. Guess what?"

"What?"

"I'm on my way to being a Pittsburgh Pirate fan," he said.

"I won't follow you that far."

∼

DEAN D'AMICO'S DESK WAS DEVOID of papers and files. Jesus seemed even more somber in the El Greco. A gentle snow was falling on the courtyard outside the window. He had a surprising smile on his face, as if something unexpectedly pleasant had happened just before I came into the room. The smile didn't help me relax as I sat down. Instead, I took a deep breath.

"Thanks for seeing me, Father."

"I only have a few moments, Mr. James. A friend just invited me to lunch in town. What is it?"

"I've decided that I don't have a vocation. I'd like to leave the seminary as soon as possible."

The smile shrunk into a deep frown. The dean looked up at Jesus.

"I believe you told me you have a devotion to the Passion."

"No, Father. You told me of yours."

"I see," he said. "I must have you confused with another. I'm saddened that you haven't found such a devotion here."

I realized this was not a line of discourse that would help me with my mission. "I'm certain now that I really didn't have a vocation at all."

"You've not given the notion a very long test, Mr. James."

"I've spent a lot of time in chapel, seeking an answer through prayer," I said, even though I knew it was a lie that I would have to take to confession.

"Does your father know of your decision?"

"My father died six years ago."

He reddened. "I see. I must have you confused with another again."

"Yes, Father."

"Does your mother know?"

"I hope to have permission to phone her after our meeting."

"I see. You're not willing to give this decision more time?"

I was feeling stronger and stronger as the discussion carried on. I was feeling that this could be the moment I missed six years ago looking at my father's coffin. I might have confronted each one of those men behind me in church, with their well-meaning advice, and grown because of that. But I hadn't been ready. I was now.

"No, Father. I've made up my mind."

"In that case, Mr. James, I'll make the necessary arrangements. And, yes, you have permission to telephone your mother."

"Thank you, Father."

"Good day, Mr. James. I must be on my way."

I left his office quickly. Instead of going to the telephone to call my mother, I walked down the long hallway and turned into the chapel. I was alone in the vast marbled space. I went to the side altar, where the older seminarian would kneel with outstretched arms, and looked at the bearded, fatherly face of St. Joseph. I felt a strength I had never felt before, a serenity that seemed to flow from thought and action rather than dreamy wanderings. My life was mine to make now, to answer the simple, yet truly human question: "What's your passion?"

And I was on my way.

Draft Dodger?

1

THE PAVILION WAS A white, classical structure with open walls lit by large, colourful lanterns and strung with streamers and decorations. A banner with bold letters stretched over the length of the entrance: **Congratulations Class of '67**. The graduates and their dates were up on the dance floor, whirling around with the music, gyrating and spinning, the women holding up their long gowns, the men stripping off their jackets, everyone smiling and singing along. In a far corner, a small circle of serious drinkers huddled over a table and held out Dixie cups for shots of gin. Dan saw his professor and wound through the crowd towards him. Dr. Wood was a short man with thick black hair and bushy eyebrows wearing a black velvet jacket and a neat bow tie.

"About your paper, Mr. James," said Dr. Wood.

"Yes, sir?"

"Where did you get those ideas?"

"From class. You talked about the deaths, the shell shock, all of it."

"As they relate to the poetry."

"But they were real."

"We're studying poetry, not reality."

Dan looked at the lanterns hanging over the dance floor. He took comfort in the soft, rosy light, away for a moment from the professor's penetrating eyes.

"I thought it was important to make the point about life."

"The point of my class, my boy," said Dr. Wood, "is literature."

"I guess I'm more interested in life."

Dr. Wood seemed to soften. "I gave you the best grade in the class, though. And I do hope you go on to grad school.

"I don't think so, Dr. Wood."

"You could be a brilliant scholar."

"I'd rather be a community organizer. I'm going into VISTA."

"VISTA? What's that?"

"Volunteers in Service to America. The domestic Peace Corps."

"I see."

"They're sending me to Chicago. I've not told anyone yet."

"Then let me be the first to wish you the best."

"Thank you, sir. That means a lot to me."

Dr. Wood, in a manly gesture, put his arm on Dan's shoulder and gave it a vigorous squeeze. He turned then and walked away.

Dan went to the bar and ordered three glasses of wine, and then left the pavilion and wandered down the hill towards the river. He approached Diana and Nick on a picnic blanket, handed glasses to them, and sat down with his. The blanket was in a field of wildflowers overlooking the river. Beyond the slowly moving river, the hills, a massive presence on the landscape, rose higher and higher, smoothly undulating towards the blue mountains of Appalachia. There was a mist rising over the land bringing with it a soft, vague melancholy.

"I love those hills," said Nick.

"We all do now," said Diana.

"And soon they'll belong to someone else."

They sat in silence for a while. Diana was slim and tall with blue eyes and an elastic, moveable face; her hair was pulled into a ponytail and tied with a satin ribbon that matched the shade of her blue gown. Nick, short and burly with broad shoulders and clean, strong features, was wearing a tuxedo.

"This is it," said Nick.

"It?" asked Dan.

"The end."

"Don't be so morbid," Diana said.

"Morbid," said Nick. "So strong and Southern. My mother calls me many things, but nothin' so fine as morbid."

"I'm not your mother," she said.

"Thank God for that." He leaned over, cupped her cheek in his hand, and kissed her.

"Don't," she said.

"Ah, cuttin' me off."

"Don't talk like that, Nick. We're having a picnic, trying to enjoy our last days together."

"Last days," he said. "Sounds like some sad, Southern song."

There was silence then as they sipped wine in the fragrant field. The sun was going down behind them, outlining the hills on the other side of the river cleanly and distinctly. Dan pulled a paperback out of his coat pocket.

"What are you reading?" asked Diana.

"Poetry."

"Brooke?" asked Nick.

"No. He's too sentimental."

"Who, then?"

"Wilfred Owen."

"Why him?"

"He got it straight about the Great War. It was ugly, horrible."

"He served, didn't he?" said Nick. He seemed irritated and turned away. He looked up the hill to the brightly lit pavilion.

"What's wrong?" asked Diana.

"I'm tired," said Nick.

"Why?"

"I had a bad dream last night."

"What was it about?"

"My dad. And God, I don't even remember him. He died when I was a kid. He was there in my dream though, wearin' his uniform. And he comes up to me and puts his arm around me and hugs me hard and, God, Diana, I felt so proud. But then he starts in yellin' and screamin' about my mom, and I wake up like a shot."

"I'm sorry, Nick."

"Sorry? You can't be sorry about a dream. It's just made me tired."

"It's the war," said Dan. "It's everywhere now."

"Maybe," said Nick. "They're killin' our boys in mean and nasty ways."

"My dad says they don't respect human life," said Diana.

Dan turned away for a moment. The trunks of the birch trees

down on the riverbank were sharp and silver in the setting sun. He looked back at Nick then. "That's what they said about the Germans in the First World War."

"Well, maybe it's true."

"It's propaganda, Nick. I wrote about it in my paper for Dr. Wood. He talked about it in class. Remember?"

"He gets carried away."

"Carried away? He's brilliant."

"I'm not talkin' about brilliance. I'm talkin' about gettin' carried away. He goes on and on about things, smokin' his cigarettes, almost settin' himself on fire."

"Listen," said Dan. "They made the Germans into animals and we're doing the same with the Vietnamese."

"So? What's the point?"

"Owen called it 'the Old Lie.' The way to get young men off to war."

Diana had remained quiet, listening, sitting with serenity. She stood up then. She walked away from the blanket and began to pick wildflowers. Nick and Dan fell silent, watching. Diana slipped a flower into her hair, came back to the blanket, and stood over them.

"I wish you wouldn't fight."

Nick looked at her and smiled, but turned to Dan again. "You keep talkin' about poets. My friends back home are talkin' about fightin' for their country."

Dan felt something snap. "I'm a friend, too. And I'm telling you that you're wrong."

"And I'm telling you that your peacenik ideas are wrong."

"I'm not a peacenik," Dan said. "I'm just a friend."

"You're not listening, Danny," said Diana. "Nick's not talking about politics."

"It's sentimental crap."

"That's enough, Danny," said Diana.

"It's true," Dan said.

"You're ruining our picnic." Diana still stood above them. She seemed to be keeping score.

"Look," said Nick. "My friends are goin' and they'll be the best soldiers they can be and, I tell you, they're gonna help save this country and you're gonna have to thank them."

"We'll see."

Dan got up and walked back up the hill towards the pavilion. He stood in the entrance in the coming darkness and looked at the dance floor to see his classmates whirling around with delight. He turned around again and saw his friends. They were coming up from the field of wildflowers, talking quickly and intensely. When they reached the patio, Diana hurried by, not looking up, and disappeared into the pavilion.

"Hey, Nick."

Nick stopped. "I wanted to talk about this at our little picnic," he said, pulling out an envelope.

"What is it?" asked Dan.

Nick turned and faced the darkening hills.

"It's my draft notice."

"They can't draft a student."

"I didn't register as a student," said Nick.

"What?"

"It's not fair for me to be treated one way and my friends down home another."

"But that's what deferments are for."

"There shouldn't be deferments," said Nick. "The rules should be the same for everybody."

"Let me see it."

Nick gave him the letter. Dan held it with shaky hands, reading slowly, feeling his lips moving slightly as he read. "They make you sound like a number. It's all wrong, Nick. Can't you see?"

"No, I can't."

"Did you tell Diana?"

"No."

"You didn't talk about it?"

"That's what I said."

"I don't understand."

"Then you don't understand women."

"Did you tell your mother?" asked Dan.

"I didn't tell her a thing. My mother never understood about the world beyond the house after my dad died. She doesn't know a thing about Vietnam. She only knows that other mothers are sending their sons off to fight communism."

Diana came back to the patio, bright and alive with the energy of the dance.

"Dan and I were just talkin' about women and war."

"Don't joke," Dan said.

"What's going on?" asked Diana.

"Nick got his notice from the draft board."

Diana stood speechless.

The music in the pavilion stopped. The men and women gathered around the stage, where Dr. Wood began to speak to the semicircle in soft, nostalgic tones. The three friends remained on the patio just beyond the light of the pavilion, distanced from the good feelings swelling inside.

Dan took Nick's arm, squeezing tightly.

"You can't go," he said.

"I've been called."

"There's Canada."

Nick pulled away from the tight grip. "How can you say that? It's treason."

"It's not treason. It's just good sense."

"I want to go. I want to be with my friends."

"Nick, this isn't about friends. They're propping up a phoney government with our lives."

"They're fightin' communism."

"That's a slogan, not the truth."

"Please," Diana said, moving between them. "That's enough."

She took Nick's arm and led him from the patio to the pavilion. They eased into the crowd around Dr. Wood. Dan stood in the dark watching the smiling, excited faces of his classmates, the warm colours of the lanterns, the flickering candles on the tables, and then he turned and walked down towards the river. Looking up he saw the hills—dark shapes now against the deep purple sky lit by a rising moon; dark shapes moving into the distance, the line of hill and horizon, harsh and true. When he reached the river, he stopped to inhale the sweet smell, yearning for some special sign of life, but instead caught the stench of chemicals dumped into the river upstream. He turned back to the bright pavilion and realized that in a matter of mere weeks he'd be away from the hills and the river and in a gritty neighbourhood in Chicago.

2

The waitress wound through the tavern with a tray, slapping last-call beers on the tables. The men around Dan and Graham were wearing flannel shirts, blue jeans, and caps with feed mill and implement logos. The band had finished the set and the room was filled with the wild talk of closing time. A huge American flag formed the backdrop of the stage, red and white stripes glaring under spotlights. The waitress reached their table. She set down two drafts and began to finger change from a cup on her tray. Graham waved her away. A burly man with a drooping moustache reached for the waitress, took her by the arm, and tried to order a round of beers. As she shook her head sternly, anger pulled his moustache into a straight line. The mood of the crowd hardened as she worked her way back to the bar. Then the band bounced back on the stage. After the players settled behind their instruments, the leader caressed the microphone.

"Please rise," he said.

The men heaved to their feet and stood swaying with suddenly serious faces. Graham rose with them. The bandleader pressed the microphone to his lips and, in a low, sensuous voice, began the national anthem. Dan remained seated. The anthem rose hoarsely around him and then, as the room roared towards the last line, the line about the land of the free and home of the brave, Dan felt a heavy hand on his shoulder.

"Get up, hippie."

The man with the moustache dug his large, thick fingers into Dan's collarbone. The pressure on his shoulder and the stares of the men around him became one sharp sensation. The pressure eased suddenly. The hand curled into a fist and rose high above his head.

"Now!" demanded the man.

Graham suddenly grabbed Dan's arm and rushed him into the sulphurous Chicago night.

3

THE DEMONSTRATORS CIRCLED THE square in front of the Federal Building holding a large banner with bright red letters: **Hell No We Won't Go!** Away from the circle, near the entrance to the building, the leaders were working out the order of speakers. A policeman was on the roof of the low-rise building across the square taking photos with a telescopic camera. A helicopter whirred above, dancing up and down, stirring the hot, humid air.

Dan and Graham were in the crowd holding a smaller banner with stark black letters: **Get Out of Nam!** Suddenly, the riot squad emerged from the alley beside the low-rise building, marching in a wedge, beating nightsticks on clear plastic shields, a terrifying and intimidating sound.

"Let's get out of here!" Graham dropped his end of the banner.

"No," said Dan. "I'm staying."

"When are you going to learn?"

Graham darted across the square and disappeared down another alley. Dan burrowed into the circle of demonstrators but kept his eye on that alley. Within moments, the riot squad reached the demonstration and cracked into it, nightsticks circling above their heads, striking randomly at the men and women. After breaking the loose circle, the wedge splintered into several striking groups, and with red and contorted faces the squad members chased the demonstrators. One of them caught a girl with jet-black hair and splattered blood across her pale face with the crack of a nightstick against the side of her head. Dan raced to escape, and made it to the alley and safety.

4

Dan moved down the breakwater in the darkness, looking for her. The cement was cold under his bare feet as the water washed over the surface. He stopped, saw the pile of clothes, and picked them up. He crouched down and called for her. The soft touch of a cold hand on his shoulder shocked him. He reared up. Peg was standing there, slim with narrow hips and small breasts, her long brown hair slick against her head and shoulders, the cream tone of her skin stunning in the close darkness. He looked away.

"Where's Graham?" she asked.

"He went back to the car," he said.

"I'm glad you stayed."

"You should get dressed."

"I'm wet," she said, moving closer.

The clothes in his hand carried the sweet, lingering scent of her.

"I hated that demonstration," she said.

"We had to do it."

"Why?"

"We had to make a statement."

"Statement? Forty people walking in a circle in front of the Federal Building?"

As they watched the small bobbing light on the mast of a sailboat slip towards the shore, she moved closer still.

"I hated the party after, too," she said. "I hate it when all the VISTAs get together to drink and do dope. I'm glad you're not like them."

Dan looked out at the water. The cloud cleared and the moon dappled the surface with silver ripples, but then another cloud crossed and covered the moon, turning the silver ripples into black water again.

"Why don't you put your clothes on now?"

"Why don't you take yours off?"

"Don't be ridiculous."

"Don't you know about free love?"

"Since when is love free?"

"If love isn't, what is?" Peg wrapped her arms around his neck and pressed into him, her skin dry now, and smooth and cool. She moved her hands from his neck to his back and began stroking.

She pulled away.

"You're priceless! I'm standing here like this and you're not doing a thing. You wouldn't make it a day in Southern California."

"I've got principles."

"And now you've got me."

5

They were the only white people in the tavern, sitting in a booth along the wall eating ribs. The tavern was dark and cool but the faces of the men at the bar were tired and irritated. The door opened, slashing light across the dirty floor, and a small, nervous man approached their table. He had anxious, yellowing eyes.

"You meetin'?"

"Sort of," Dan said.

"You got you a five?"

Dan reached into his pocket. "Here you go."

The man took the bill and hurried out of the tavern.

"Why, Danny?" asked Peg. Her long brown hair fell on her sharp shoulders. "It just goes for dope."

"We're buddies."

"That's not what VISTA is all about," she said.

"What is it all about?"

"The draft," said Graham.

"Bullshit," Dan said.

"We're here because we didn't want to go to Nam. VISTA gave us deferments, but the lottery eliminates that. We're fucked, to put it bluntly."

"I'm not."

"Don't be impossible. You don't want to go there any more than I do."

"We'll see."

Peg slid her warm, dry hand into Dan's. "Don't talk like that. I can't handle it, not with the baby coming. "

"I thought we weren't telling anybody yet."

"It came up. I'm sorry."

"I see."

Draft Dodger?

"You don't see." Peg turned in her chair. "We're friends. He has a right to know about the baby."

Graham put his elbows on the table. The turquoise stone on the silver band on his wrist caught light from a neon sign and, as he twisted his wrist, it became bright blue. "I made my decision," he said. "I'm going to Canada."

"What?"

"We could go, too," said Peg.

"I don't believe this," Dan said. "You two have got this all planned."

"You're going to have a baby," said Graham. "You've got to grow up."

"Stick it, Graham."

"Please, the two of you," said Peg. Tears came quietly, and mascara ran down her pale cheeks. Graham reached into his pocket and pulled out a handkerchief to give to her. Dan gripped his mug of beer, holding his hand on the coolness, and then took a long, deep drink. Out of the silence, Marvin Gaye erupted from the jukebox.

"I need time," Dan said.

"You're out of time," said Graham. "The lottery took care of that. I'm leaving for Canada next month, but it'll take two months to get your papers organized. You'll have to find a place and get a job."

"I can't change the whole direction of my life over ribs in a bar."

"Okay," said Graham. "Just don't be surprised when your induction notice comes."

Peg pushed away from the table, stood up, and spread her slender, long fingers on the tabletop. She seemed on the verge of shouting, but instead hurried to the back of the tavern. As Graham wiped his hands with a napkin, Dan caught the bartender's eye. He came to the table, a tall, robust man wearing an apron.

"Big rap, man."

"We're meeting," Dan said.

"You be meetin' all da time."

"Yea, we got that one down."

The bartender slapped a draft on the table and wound away. Peg came back to the table.

"Are you okay?" asked Graham.

"No," she said. "I was sick."

"We should go," said Graham.

"No," she said. "We have to finish this."

Dan took a drink from the fresh mug of beer.

"What have you decided?" Peg's tone was clean and cold. There was no Marvin Gaye on the jukebox now to break the silence.

"I asked a question," said Peg.

"Let's go," Dan said. He stood up and went to the bar and pulled out a ten-dollar bill. The bartender took the money and punched the cash register. "Where you goin', man?"

Dan looked at him. "Canada."

"What?"

"I'm joking," Dan said.

"Canada takes all those draft dodgers, man."

"That right?"

"You bet, man. You stay put and have some ribs with the folks. Then, see a little Nam."

Dan looked down the dark aisle and saw them by the door. Graham held his hand firmly in the centre of her back. He pushed the door open and led her into the slashing light. And then they were gone.

"Change," said the bartender.

Dan looked back at him and felt a flush rushing to his face.

"Change?"

The bartender pointed to the bills and coins on the bar. But Dan turned away and pushed through the door into the hard Chicago sun.

6

THE STATION WAGON IDLED in the queue, a vehicle away from a uniformed man with a moustache standing in front of the customs kiosk, his hands comfortably clasped behind him. A long, low building backed into a neatly landscaped hill. Dan glanced into the rear-view mirror and saw beyond the Peace Bridge, on the other side of the river, the decaying buildings of Buffalo. He looked at Peg, who was twisting her wedding ring around and around.

"You okay?"

"No," she said. "I'm not ready for this."

"It's our only option."

"Your only option," she said.

He pulled ahead then and stopped at the kiosk.

"Visitors?"

"No, sir," Dan said. "We're immigrating."

The man pointed to the low building behind him.

"You'll have to see an officer."

Dan pulled over and reached for the manila envelope with their immigration papers. The sun was beginning to set, dusting the yellow leaves on the hill behind the building.

"You want me to do the talking?"

"I don't care," she said.

They got out and went into the office. It was only a few minutes before they came back into the setting sun. Dan gave one of the stamped cards to Peg and looked at his card again. The stamp was simple: within the crest of Canada, the date and the place of immigration. They got into the car and pulled onto the highway to Toronto.

"It's going to work," Dan said.

"It's easy for you to say that. But I don't know a single soul in the whole country."

"There'll be other draft dodgers."
"I hate that term."
"You know Graham."
"Yes," she said. "I know Graham."

They drove on in silence then, into the heartland of Canada, moving by tidy farms and fields in the descending dusk, listening to the radio. After a while, she seemed to relax, her hands resting easily in her lap, her tight lips softening. He moved his hand from the steering wheel to the back of her seat and touched her thin shoulder. She did not move under his touch. She looked into the headlights, driving into the dark, and eased into a calm, mellow smile.

"Thank God for Graham," she said.

Like neon in the coming night, the words pulsed with clarity and insistence. He removed his hand from her shoulder. They said nothing as the highway edged to the east and the glow of the city hovered in the clear night. As they entered the canopy of light, she continued to stare into the headlights with that calm, mellow smile.

7

Dan looked across the surface of the lake to the round green islands. The sun was high and hot and the air clean and cool. Peg flicked the sand with her toes and rolled over, her brown hair slick against her neck and shoulders. The sand speckled her bare back and made swirls on her blue bathing suit. He reached for her. The skin was hot and taut over the sharpness of her shoulder blades. She tensed under his touch.

"Not now," she said.

"What?"

"You know what."

"You didn't mind before."

"That was before. We're married now and I'm having a baby."

She stood up, waded into the water, and dove, disappearing into the lake. When she reached the diving platform, she climbed the ladder and sat down, raising her face to the sun. He followed her. He swam to the far side of the platform and swung himself up, pulling it down with his weight. She turned, her eyes brown and startled.

"It's you," she said.

He scrambled across the platform and sat down next to her. The bathing suit clung to her breasts, rounder and fuller with the coming baby. On the beach, a young mother was spreading a towel on the sand. Two blond, robust children ran from her to splash in the lapping edge of the lake.

"They're so cute," said Peg. She drew her legs up, crossed her arms around them, and watched the woman walk to the edge of the water. "But she's lost her shape. I hope it never happens to me."

He reached around and ran his hand down the sleek bathing suit. She stood up.

"I told you," she said.

"This is our honeymoon, Peg."

"You already had your honeymoon." She held her hands on her hips, her long fingers spread across the bulge of her tummy. "You already put a baby in there."

"The baby's not nearly due."

"I can't help that. I can't help that at all."

He stood up. He was close to her now, close to her swelling breasts, aware of the high cut of the blue bathing suit on her hips.

"You mean I'm cut off."

"That's your kind of term."

"Do you mean that, though?"

"I just know that I'm having a baby. That's what I know."

He shifted his weight, swaying the platform.

"Let's talk," he said.

"Talk about what? I'm pregnant. I'm in a strange country. I miss my family. Graham understands."

"What does he understand?"

"Me."

"What about you?"

"He understands that I'm having a baby and I'm afraid and I'm homesick."

"Does he know that you've decided not to have sex with me?"

"Yes, he does."

"You talk about our sex life?"

"I talk about whatever I want to talk about. He knows how to listen."

"He has no right to know this."

"He has the right to a lot more," she said.

She turned and dove. He watched her surface and then slip out of the water, walk up the beach, and disappear into the woods. He dove then and reached the shallows. The woman on the beach smiled at him.

"Hello," she said.

He pulled his fingers through his beard, feeling the cold water drip down his chest.

"Their father's fishing," she said, pointing to a boat near one of the islands.

Draft Dodger?

"The fishing's good?"

"Oh, yeah," said the woman. "I'll be cleaning them all afternoon."

They stood awkwardly together, looking towards the boat.

"Your wife went back to the campsite."

"I guess she did," he said.

"She's so lovely."

The children splashed towards their mother, circled her, and held on to her thighs, looking shyly at the stranger.

"You got kids?"

"No," he said.

"That's the way to go when you're young."

He looked towards the islands again.

"You from around here?" she asked.

"No," he said. "We're living in Toronto, but we're from the States originally."

"How long have you been in Canada?"

"Just a little while."

"Do you like it?"

"I do."

"You seem so happy."

He shifted his gaze from the islands to the water.

"Why did you come?" she asked.

"It was the war."

"The war?"

"Vietnam," he said.

"Oh," she said. She leaned down to one of the blond children, but looked up at him.

"Draft dodger?"

"I guess I am."

She pulled her lips into a tight, thin line.

"It must be hard on her."

He kept his eyes on the water.

"Coming to a strange country. Leaving her family. It must be hard." She pointed to the boat. "I'm glad their father doesn't have to go."

"Yeah."

"Well," said the woman. "I better get these little ones back for their nap." She gathered the children, fetched their things, and disappeared down the road.

Dan turned towards the water, dove, and swam with a manic fury, tearing away from the shore, alone in the vastness of the lake, until finally he stopped, spent. As he looked across the lake, the islands rose from the surface like the burial mounds in the countryside around his home in southern Ohio.

8

THE NURSE FASTENED DAN's surgical gown and ushered him into the labour room.

"She's got a ways to go so we gave her something to relax her a bit so she can rest between contractions." The nurse left the room.

"How you doing, hon?"

Her eyes focused on him.

"How could you?" The anger in her voice became thinning lips, squinting eyes.

"What?"

"How could you wear that old shirt when I'm having my baby?"

"Peg, it's a surgical gown. They wouldn't let me in without it."

She closed her eyes then, arching her back and moaning, white fists digging into the sides of her belly.

"Is there anything I can do?"

"You've already done this," she said.

"This?"

"I want to be home," she shot back. "I want to be with my mother. Can't you understand that?"

"You know we can't risk going to the States."

"We? You're the one who dodged the draft. You're the one who can't go home."

He looked out the window. The clouds were closer now, heavier.

"Has Graham phoned?"

"No," he said. "I keep trying, but he's never in his office."

"Oh, I wish he were here."

She turned her head away from him, breathing hard and fast, digging her fists deeper into her belly. Anger tightened her face.

"You're the one who wanted natural childbirth," she said. She began to sob, breaking the rhythm of her breathing, gasping, heaving up and down, moving roughly. "Get my mother. Get Graham. Get somebody!"

"I'm getting the nurse."

Dan hurried out of the room and down the hall to the nursing station. The nurse was in front of the counter, reading a magazine.

"She's upset and she's not making any sense."

"They never do," said the nurse.

"Is she okay? What can I do?"

"She's fine. But she's got five, six more hours. Nothing you can do. You'd be better off at home."

"Home?"

"We'll call you."

"I didn't think it would be like this."

"They never do," she said. "Go home."

The nurse turned him around, untied the gown, and pulled it away from him. Through the window, he saw large, swirling flakes of snow falling on the wide white landscape. As he looked towards the dull grey horizon, he tried to remember the sound of his father's voice.

9

Peg was lying on the diving board in the shade of the old and heavy palms, dangling her slender leg over the side. She was lithe and lean in a new blue bikini, as fresh as a teenager. Dan was sitting by the side of the pool, swishing his feet in the warm water. Peg sat up.

"I hope he didn't have trouble at the border."

"We didn't."

"But he got his induction notice."

"We're both draft dodgers."

"You didn't get an induction notice."

"I don't want to argue," he said.

"Well, why are you then? You always say that and just go right ahead."

Dan slipped into the pool, swam towards the diving board, and leapt up, reaching for her leg. She jerked away and wrapped her arms around her knees. But he swished down into the water and roared up, grabbing the diving board with his hands, pulling himself up.

"You're such a fucking child."

She marched off the diving board into the house. He began to swim then, back and forth, keeping his head down and his eyes closed, rhythmically smacking the surface of the water. Finally, he climbed out and sat down on the hot cement, breathing hard. She came out of the house with a tall glass.

"What's that?"

"A gin and tonic."

"Peg, it's only eleven.

"I'm in my father's house and I'll have a drink if I want to."

Dan got up and followed her to the table and chairs on the patio behind the pool. She set the drink down on the table, opened the umbrella, and tilted it to shade the chairs. Then she sat down and sipped on the drink. He went behind the chair and placed his hand on her warm, thin shoulder. She twitched away.

"Don't start that," she said.

"Start what?"

"You know what."

"I just touched you," he said.

"I am not a sex object."

Dan sat down on the chair facing her, water still dripping from his swimsuit, and rubbed his hands up and down his legs.

"What's the matter?"

"I told you," she said. "I need some space for myself."

The back door opened and her mother came around the pool to the patio. She was a small, delicate woman.

"The baby's down," she said. "And your friend has arrived."

Peg tore from the chair and ran across the patio and into the house. Her mother looked at him.

"She's got so much energy."

"She does."

"And he's such a fine young man."

Dan looked away from her and stared into the blue water.

"He's from New England?"

"He is."

"I thought so," she said. "He's so well spoken, so polite. Have you known him long?"

"Since Chicago," he said. "We were on the same project."

"He's not in Toronto anymore?"

"No," he said. "He went to work in northern Ontario."

"That sounds so romantic."

They came out of the house, her arm tucked intimately into his. Graham was wearing khakis and a cotton shirt and carrying a bouquet of white wildflowers. He handed the flowers to her mother with a comic, charming bow.

"I'll find a vase," she said. "And leave you three alone to catch up on old times."

They moved to the table and sat.

"What's it like?" said Peg.

Graham twisted the band on his wrist so the turquoise stone caught the sun.

"It's great," he said. "I love the north. The landscape. The people."

"What's the project?" asked Dan.

"We're doing a land claim for the local Indian band."

"Land claim?"

"We're trying to prove that they still hold title to the land through the treaty they signed. And we're building a good case."

"That's exciting," said Peg.

"What's with you guys?"

"I'm still at the settlement house," Dan said. "Peg's home with the baby. The same old shit."

Graham stretched his legs and raised his hands behind his head.

"We missed you." Peg reached over and touched the turquoise stone on his wrist. Then she reached further for her drink. She drained it.

"Make me another, honey."

"It's not even noon, Peg."

"Make one for Graham, too."

Dan got up slowly and walked around the pool to the house. The air was sharp and cool inside. He went through the kitchen to his father-in-law's small den. The walls were lined with bookshelves and the furniture was old and comfortable. He mixed the drinks at the liquor cabinet. He could hear her parents talking quietly, trying not to disturb the baby. Through the windowpane, he could see the two of them on the patio. She was talking with her hands, waving her long fingers in wide, animated circles. He returned to the patio with the drinks.

"So what's so bad about the work at the settlement house, Dan?"

Dan sat down in front of them. "It's okay, but I really miss the fuck-it-all attitude of the ghetto."

"How can you say that?" Peg turned, the drink swishing in her glass. "I hated every second in that dirty place."

"The people were good, Peg."

"The people are good in Toronto, too."

"I'm not saying they aren't. I'm saying they're different."

"You're the one who's different."

Graham stood up and walked to the edge of the pool. "I've got some news."

"Tell us," said Peg.

"We've been asked to put together a project in Toronto."

"Who's we?" asked Peg.

"Jamie and I. She's my boss. She's been a community organizer for years."

"I see," said Peg. She began to rub her finger up and down the side of the glass.

"And there may be some open spots."

"Oh, wow," said Peg.

"I told Jamie about you guys. Maybe we could work together again."

"Oh, Danny. We could, couldn't we?"

Dan looked up at the shrouded sky. "What about the baby?"

"She can go to daycare."

"Let's think about it."

"It would be so exciting."

"What about my job?"

"You hate your job. We could be back together again. Just like Chicago. With Jamie, of course."

"We'll see."

"Hey," said Graham. "When's a guy get a swim around here?"

Peg stood up and ran her hands down her narrow hips, slowly licking her lips.

"Now," she said. She grabbed him by the arm, catching him by surprise, and pulled him into the pool. They splashed and surfaced. She was wrapped around him now, laughing, her voice ringing like a clear, sharp bell. And, as they sank into the water again, the sudden appearance of the California sun sharpened the silence.

10

Dan turned from the highway onto the gravel road that wound along the racing northern river. The sun was going down, splashing scarlet on the stark stands of birch. In front of them, a man came out of the woods carrying a string of sparkling trout; he was trailed by two small girls wearing tired sundresses. Dan slowed down, stopped beside the man, and rolled down the window.

"Is the Land Claim Centre far?"

The man nodded and pointed his wiry brown arm.

They continued down the gravel road and soon the lake opened ahead, broad and black, dotted with round green islands. Within moments he saw the house on a rise above the lake in a stand of tall pines, with furniture and boxes stacked on either side of the front steps. He turned to Peg. She was sleeping with the baby curled into her arms.

"We made it," he said.

She stirred, but did not open her eyes.

He pulled up in front of the house and got out of the car. Inside the open door, he saw a woman, pert and blond with her hair pulled into a ponytail. She wore a Levi's jacket over a white cotton dress. She came down the front steps, smiling warmly, her green eyes clear.

"Is Graham around?" he asked.

"No," she said. "He's gone to town. Can I help you?"

"We're his friends from Toronto."

She smiled quickly and easily, and extended her hand. The grip was strong and firm.

"I'm Jamie," she said. "You must be Dan."

Peg got out of the car then.

When he introduced them, Jamie reached out and touched the baby's bare arm.

"Isn't she a darling?"

"She's a sleeping darling now," said Peg.

"I've got a place ready for her upstairs. Let's settle her in."

Peg followed her into the house.

Dan got the bags from the back of the station wagon, set them down by the steps, and went around the house to the rise above the lake. On an island near the centre of the lake, etched softly in the evening slant of the sun, he saw smoke rising from the shore. Darkness settled in, and the only sound was the rhythmic knocking of the pines. He took the bags into the house.

An oil lamp on a table lit the front room. The space was lined with empty bookcases and filled with packing boxes. Oddly, there was one book on the empty shelves. He picked it up and looked at the cover: *Seven Storey Mountain,* by Thomas Merton.

"Do you know it?" Jamie had come like a faint wind, a scent of something fresh and green.

"Yeah," he said. "I read it a long time ago."

She touched the spine of the book. "He thought about becoming an organizer," she said. "But went to the monastery instead."

"I was there," he said.

"At Gethsemane?"

"Yeah," he said. "And I couldn't figure out why he chose that over organizing in Harlem."

"I know more about organizing than I do about monasteries, but it's a good question."

He began to turn the pages of the book, trying to deflect the quiet intensity next to him, to turn it away. She shook out her ponytail and drew her fingers through her hair.

"I've been doing this a long time," she said. "In Alberta, Newfoundland, up here. But, sometimes I wonder if maybe there's another, quieter, way."

"When I was in the garden at the monastery in Kentucky, it was very quiet. Peaceful." He put the book down and eased away from her.

"What can I do to help?" he asked.

"Do you mind packing?"

"I've done a lot of that."

"Well, that means we'll probably get along."

"Yeah," he said. "We'll probably get along."

Peg came down the stairs, looking at them intently. Her leg brushed the table and the oil lamp tipped over. Oil flew across the floor, creating a pathway of flame. Peg screamed and rushed out the front door. Dan was frozen for a long moment as the flame moved across the dry wooden floor. He started for the stairs, but Jamie grabbed his arm and held it hard.

"Stop," she said. Taking off her denim jacket, she methodically beat at the pathway of flame. Suddenly, it seemed, the room was in darkness.

A flashlight beam slashed towards the front door as Peg rushed in. She walked into the sharp circle of light. "The baby!"

"It's okay, it's out. Jamie smothered the flames with her jacket."

"What happened?"

"You knocked the lamp down," he said.

"I got so scared. I didn't think about the baby. I'm not used to lamps."

"We were all scared, I think, but it's okay now," said Jamie.

Dan looked at the beam of light that illuminated him and Peg, and the woman behind it. The smell of flame was mixed with the sound of wind soughing through the pines in the northern blackness. There was no uniformed man or stamped documents, but Dan was fairly sure he'd crossed another border.

11

Dan left their apartment in the Beach. The air in the hallway was close and thick with the smells of summer dinners. He took the stairs and reached the ground floor. The trees in front of the building were full and heavy, hanging down and holding the hot, humid air. He turned towards the lake, walking by couples sitting on their large stone and cement verandas. The dark presence of the lake was just beyond the bushes at the end of the street.

Jamie was sitting there under a street lamp, reading a paperback. She was wearing a simple cotton dress and sandals.

She stood up. "This is so clandestine."

"I couldn't think of anything better. What are you reading?"

"John Donne's poetry. I thought it might be fitting preparation for an evening out. Very metaphysical."

"Is that what we are—metaphysical?"

She shrugged.

They pushed through an opening in the bushes to the beach. The air was cooler and the darkness was serious and complete. They fell into step on the boardwalk.

"So, what did you tell her?"

"I said I was going out."

"With me?"

"I wasn't that precise."

"But she knows?"

"We've agreed to try this open marriage thing. She went out, too. I got the babysitter."

"Did she say who she was going out with?"

"She wasn't that precise."

"That's very open."

They listened for a while to their sandals slapping on the wooden slats. Suddenly, Jamie jumped down and, picking up a stick, drew a circle in the sand. And, with a flourish, divided the circle with the wavy line that transformed it into the mystical symbol for man and woman. She sat within half of the circle.

"Come," she said.

He entered the circle and crouched down.

"Sit." She giggled. "I didn't mean it to sound like an order."

Dan sat, facing her, hugging his knees, as she did hers.

"I'm primed for this evening with Donne, remember?" she said. "Metaphysical love. So, what we have here is the universal sign for yin and yang, two cosmic forces that together make the world go round, each element containing the seed of the other."

"As I recall, the dark side of the circle is generally considered the masculine force."

"Which has within it the seed of the female force," said Jamie. "It's about balance. Within individuals, between people, in life generally."

"I'm a bit short of the masculine force, I think. Raised in a household of women, took on lots of feminine energy."

"A big white eye in the black side, then. Balance, Dan. It's about owning what you are so you can engage with what you need."

"I think I need you," he said.

"And maybe I need you, but that's not what this is about. This is about completing our individual selves, so we can be true partners with another . . . or not, as life delivers. Think of Merton: there's a guy who was complete unto himself."

"If Merton had been my father, I'd be a different man."

"And if Merton had been my father, I'd be a different woman. But he made a choice other than to procreate, so we're both out of luck."

Jamie jumped up, brushed the sand from her dress, and grabbed Dan's hand. "Come on, let's go up to Queen and get something to eat."

He hesitated, looked away from her to the dark water of the lake.

"Are you afraid she'll discover us?" she asked.

"No," he lied.

"Then can we?"

"Sure."

They left the boardwalk, cut across the narrow band of grass, and walked up the quiet street, leaning into each other as they talked, discovering themselves.

They sat across from each other in a booth by the window of a small restaurant on Queen Street. She drew her hands through her hair, streaked with the sun, alive and clean. They ordered drinks. When the waitress left the table, Jamie placed her hands over his and looked carefully into his eyes. Her green eyes were full of promise, honest and clean.

"I want to be clear, Dan. I like you a lot. I have hopes for our relationship. But I know there's a lot more on the line for you, and I don't want you to do anything you don't want to do. Promise me that."

"I don't know what I want to do. I'm much clearer on what I don't want."

"You'll figure it out," she said.

They ordered food, ate it, talked of many things. As they were sipping their coffee, Dan looked out the window and saw Peg. She was with Graham. He was talking and waving his large hands like a magician. And she was laughing with the wild spirit of their days in Chicago.

"What?" said Jamie, following his frozen glance. "Oh."

"Well," she said, a silence later, "I'm going." She stood, took his hand and stroked it, kissed his broad forehead, and left.

12

Dan left his office on a clear blue morning and took the streetcar back towards the Beach. He got out at Neville Park. He saw the steel blue water and the piercing blue sky and the billowing green trees and walked faster. At the pavilion, he turned east. The grass was filling with young women and babies, the beach with the men and women who lived in the apartments along the boardwalk. He walked with a clear purpose, looking ahead, sorting faces just as he sorted the papers on his desk. Until he saw them.

They were on a grey blanket with fruit and cheese and bread.

And he was on them. All he could see was their crude attempt to hide a bottle of wine at eleven thirty in the morning.

"Okay," he said.

"Jesus," said Peg.

Graham leapt to his feet. He was wearing the same clothes he had worn the night before. He was always wearing the same clothes, the same khaki pants and white cotton shirt.

Dan saw the cork, grabbed it, and pushed it into the bottle. He began to stuff things into the back of the stroller, the wine and glasses and white napkins and fruit and cheese and bread, things he had bought, things, things that she had claimed made no difference to them—they were beyond things, she would say, beyond the materialistic crap that made North America go around.

He looked at Graham.

"Go," he said.

"I . . ."

"Just go, Graham."

"It's not what—"

"Get the fuck out of here!"

This was too loud, too crude for the beach on a clear blue day in August.

"Don't go, Graham," said Peg. She was looking into his eyes as though he were the secret that danced in the darkest part of the night.

Dan felt the adrenaline pump through his chest and arms, the muscles and sinews of his legs.

"I mean it, fucker."

This was far too loud.

"Stop, Danny."

The baby started to cry. He picked her up and put her in the stroller and wheeled away, clattering across the planks of the boardwalk, the sound rising like the rumble of a streetcar.

13

Dan stumbled up the narrow stairs to the apartment. The light was harsh in the hallway and the humid heat was shot through with the stale smells of late summer. He reached the top floor and fumbled his key into the lock. He pushed in the sticking door and tumbled into the dark apartment. He staggered through the living room and dining room and turned into the small kitchen. He pulled open the fridge and took out a bottle of beer. He pawed through a drawer, looking for the opener. He found it and opened the beer. He took a long drink, and then went back towards the living room. He flicked on the light, sat down on the floor in front of the stereo, and fingered through the stack until he found a battered Crosby, Stills & Nash album. He put it on, turned up the volume, and began singing drunkenly about ones and twos and togethers.

The dining room light flicked on.

"Where have you been?"

The words had the power to evoke a deep-down, murderous anger that brought him to his feet.

"Where have I been?"

"It's two o'clock in the morning, Danny."

"I've been with my friends."

"Friends?"

"My new friends, my good friends."

"How much did you drink?"

Those words. He had started to hate those words as a small boy in his dark bedroom, when his father would burst into their home after a drinking session on payday. Those words.

"A few," he said.

"How many?"

He started towards her. She was wearing a short black nightgown.

The black straps were sharp and distinct on her tanned shoulders.
"Enough," he said.
"Where have you been?"
Those words. Those same words.
"The Silver Dollar."
"Jesus, Danny."
"What, Jesus?"
"You could get killed in that part of town."
"My friends are not going to kill me."
"They are not your friends."
"They are better friends than that motherfucker."
Peg turned on that. She flicked off the light and walked back towards the bedroom. He turned the stereo louder, and then followed her to the bedroom.
"You'll wake her," she said.
"I don't care."
"Please, Danny. It's late. She needs to sleep."
He turned on the overhead light. The light was hard and white.
"I want you to listen," he said.
"It's late."
"I want you to listen to that song. Do you remember that song? Do you remember when we met?"
Peg turned away from him and slipped under the hand-sewn quilt.
"I want to talk," he said.
She laughed. "And I want to sleep."
He went to the bed and sat down.
"Have you fucked him?"
"You are so crude."
"Have you?"
Peg sat up. "We have to talk."
"So now *she* wants to talk."
She pulled her knees together.
"Have you?" he insisted.
"This is not working."
He loomed over her.

"Tell me."

"I love him," she said. "I've made love to him."

He heaved up suddenly and his fist hammered into the wall behind her, *smack*, splitting the skin of his knuckles, and then his other fist, *smack*, and again, *smack, smack, smack*, his fists pumping into the hard white plaster. Blood, spreading in a jagged circle above her head.

"That's it." She slid from the bed and began to pull on her clothes.

"What are you doing?"

"I'm going to Graham's."

He sat down on the bed. He looked at his knuckles.

"I'm bleeding."

"Well, do something about it. Don't just talk. Do something."

She rushed away. He heard her go into the other room and pick up the baby, and then move down the hallway and slam the door behind her. The song about ones and twos and togethers echoed in his head.

14

He sat on the boardwalk watching the blue water lap on the beach. Older couples walked easily along, stopping from time to time to watch the diving gulls. And young mothers began to arrive with their carriages and picnic baskets. He felt her behind him, then. He had wound gauze around his swollen knuckles. His hands looked like white boxing gloves. She sat down next to him and gently cradled his hands on her lap.

"My wife and my child are gone."

"Did Graham take them?"

"No. She left and took the baby."

"She's gone to be with the man she loves. What's wrong with that?"

"I don't know. It didn't work out very well to be with the man she doesn't love. Not for either of us."

"People can't be blamed for falling in love. Even when it's inconvenient."

They sat together looking at the grey water meeting the grey sky.

"You can't see the horizon," Dan said.

"Yeah. Reminds me of the yin-yang symbol. You can't tell where the water meets the sky, but each is its own thing."

"You know that song?"

"Which song?"

"The one about being three together when you're for each other."

"That's a good song."

The sun suddenly emerged from behind the clouds, and the vista that was grey became blue.

"Look," said Jamie. "Now you can tell where one ends and the other begins. Just a tiny line between."

"Ah. They are three together."

There they sat, separate and together, contemplating the lake and the sky, blue on blue.

Tenderness

1

THE SUN WAS HIGH and hot on that early August day in 1909, shimmering and alive, burning the prairie grass between the barn and the farmhouse. The boy was in the shade under the eaves of the barn, hidden in the thin, dark line, his back against the rough pine boards, knees drawn up, arms curled around them. His mother was standing on the steps of the veranda wearing a simple blue housedress. She was a slight woman with long ashen hair and pale skin that never seemed to burn in the sun. She crossed her arms and looked down the long lane to the flat stretch of prairie. In the distance to the east, the grain elevators of Cayley, Alberta, looked like phantoms in the stunning heat.

The homestead was on high ground, tucked into a stand of trees at the edge of a ravine, which rose from Highwood River. The river bore down from the mountains in the distance. It sliced across the prairie and, from place to place, created parkland such as this, with clusters of pine, poplar, and pure white birch. The straight rush of the river across this part of the prairie allowed the homesteads to be cut into neat, square sections of land, which were newly planted with wheat. Beyond the prairie, ranches rose into the foothills. The farmhouse was simple and square, built with bare pine boards. The only embellishment was the veranda, with its finely turned pillars and railings.

A line of dust began to rise on the road from town, approaching soundlessly, disturbing the visual calm. His mother turned and went back into the house. The boy stood, walked across the yard, and took the veranda steps in one leap. He circled around to the south side of the house. He was fair and slight like his mother, with the same ashen hair, but his eyes were a sharp blue. He leaned on the railing, looked down the lane to the rising line of dust, and listened. A whirring broke into the stillness like the rustle of locusts. A motorcycle sped up the lane, slowed, and pulled into the yard. The thin, wiry man on the motorcycle waited for the girl on the back to jump down, then he jabbed the kickstand with his black boot. The boy went down the steps to meet them. The man wore jeans and a blackened buckskin jacket. He stuck out a dirty hand. The boy shook it.

"I'm your Uncle Joe, Luke. Remember Rachel?"

The boy considered his cousin. She was wearing brown cotton culottes, a white blouse, and high-topped shoes. She had the same arching cheekbones and black hair as his uncle, but her eyes were a deep and tranquil blue. Before he could reply, his mother came out of the house and down the steps wearing a different dress, severe and black. Joe went to her, offering his open arms. She winced, but moved into him.

"My regrets," said Joe. "It was so sudden."

Mother flinched then drew away from him.

"Are there things, Joe? Clothes and things?"

"Just what's in the bags."

"I see."

Joe turned and untied the saddlebags. He had a long, rough face and needed a shave. He handed the bags to her.

"You must be hungry."

"We are," he said. "But I need to take this down."

"Take it down?"

"I need to take the cycle apart to cool her down."

"I could hold off supper awhile."

"I'd be obliged, Mae."

Joe took the handlebars of the motorcycle in his strong, dirty hands.

"I'll use the barn."

"The barn?"

"To take the cycle down."

"Certainly."

Joe walked the motorcycle across the yard and into the dark barn. Mother turned to Rachel then reached out and rubbed her arm with sad affection.

"You're such a young lady now."

"I turned fourteen."

"And a pretty young lady, too. Like your mother."

This time Rachel flinched.

"Are there things you need, honey?"

"No, ma'am."

"Are you sure now?"

"Yes, ma'am."

"It's just like Joe to think a young lady could travel with what's in a saddlebag."

"It's summer, Aunt Mae. I'll be fine. And I got my good dress. For tomorrow."

"I see," said Mother.

She turned to Luke.

"Take Rachel down to the river while I get supper."

Mother hurried back into the house then, leaving the cousins alone.

"Do you?" asked Rachel.

"Do I what?"

"Remember me."

"I think so."

"I remember you. We got the same eyes."

Luke turned and went around the side of the house. Rachel followed him. They crossed the small vegetable garden behind the house and went into the windbreak. There was a path beaten through the scrub poplar, and inside, under the tall, waving pines, the shade was cool and enveloping. She struggled to keep up with him, and as he broke through the other side of the windbreak, she reached him and touched his bare arm. The tips of her fingers were dry, but charged with energy.

"Oh, my," she said.

They stood on the edge of a small cliff, which cascaded down to the river below. The river was narrow, but running swiftly. White stone banks edged into the deep brown soil on both sides. Beyond the river, the fields opened to prairie, stretching to the horizon. And there, faintly etched, as far as the eye could see, were the mountains. Luke took her hand and, moving ahead, found the toeholds in the side of the cliff and started down to the river below. They worked quickly and soon stood on the bank of bright white stones. Even in the heat of the late afternoon sun, the air by the water was crisp and cool. Rachel untied her shoes and started for the river.

"Careful."

She stopped and turned. The skin of her feet was rich and brown against the harsh white of the stones.

"Why?"

"She looks gentle, but the current's mean."

"Mean?"

"It'll take you away. Just like that."

Luke kicked off his shoes and went to the edge of the water. He rolled up his pant legs, sat on a large stone, and slipped his feet into the running water. She sat on a stone next to him, dappling her feet close to his.

"How did it happen?"

"What?"

"Your father," said Rachel.

"I don't know."

"You don't know?"

Luke looked up towards the farmhouse. "She won't tell me."

"She won't?"

"She said he just died and that's enough to know."

"But where?"

"He was ridin' the train to Fort William. That's what he told me when he left."

"Why was he going?"

"They had a strike goin' on down there."

"A strike?"

"Father was workin' for the union and the men down there needed help. They were startin' to shoot them down. It was in the papers."

"I see," said Rachel. She flicked her toes in the cold, running water. "Did you cry?

"About what?"

"About your father dying."

He kicked his feet in the cold water.

"Did you?"

"No," said Luke.

"I didn't cry when my mother died either. They said I should, but I didn't. And I won't. Ever."

The strange sharpness of her words brought him to his feet. He reached down, picked up some stones, and began to fling them across the surface of the river.

"Will you?"

"Will I what?"

"Will you ever cry?" asked Rachel.

Luke dropped the stone from his hand. "Let's go back."

He slipped on his shoes and started up the side of the cliff. By the time he reached the windbreak, she was at his side again. They entered the yard. Luke looked at the dark open door of the barn. Instead of going into the house, he went towards the barn. Rachel followed. Joe was leaning into the motorcycle in the murky light, and when they came into the barn, he stood up and pulled a rag from his pocket and wiped his long, blackened fingers.

"You know cycles, Luke?"

"No, sir."

"I don't suppose your father liked the cycles."

"He didn't."

"He probably liked the automobiles."

"He did."

"Now, my Kate, that was a different story."

Joe put his arm around his daughter and squeezed her shoulder with his large, rough hand.

"And my Rachel here, a different story still."

"I don't like motorcycles," she said.

"She likes the gymnastics. Right, honey?"

Rachel blushed but said nothing.

"I seen you got rings hangin' from that tree in the yard. They yours?"

"My father liked the rings," said Luke.

"He did, did he? You could show Luke some of your tricks on those rings, Rachel."

Her blush deepened, but she still said nothing.

Joe turned back to the motorcycle then, and, working quickly with a set of grease-stained wrenches, took the engine casing from the frame and set it with the other parts lined up on the barn floor. He nodded to Rachel. In one fluid motion, they lifted the frame, spun it around, and set it gently upside down. Joe went around the frame and encircled her with his arm again, digging his fingers into her soft skin.

"Now let's see if Mae can cook as good as my Kate."

Joe strode away. Rachel stood there for a moment in the shadows of the barn, rubbing the finger marks on her arm and watching her father's back, her eyes sad and knowing. They left the barn then. The sun was still high and hot, burning down on the hard earth. They reached the house and went inside. The kitchen was a long rectangle, with a table in a small alcove by the windows, which looked out on the barn. Joe was sitting at the head of the table, waiting. The table was set with the tableware reserved for special occasions. Set snugly in the alcove, the space was cosy and warm. Luke scrambled behind the table and Rachel sat down opposite him, facing the windows. Mother brought the platters of food to the table, setting them in a circle around Joe. He piled large mounds of potatoes, vegetables, and beef on the delicate plate. Mother sat down, opposite him.

"I was hopin' to take Rach down to the old trading post," he said.

"There's not much to see. The building is falling down now."

"All the same, I'd like to take her. It's where her mama was a child."

"Fine," said Mother. "You can take the automobile." She paused. "After . . . the funeral."

"I thought we'd go tonight."

"Tonight?"

"We got lots of light still."

"Fine," said Mother.

"I was thinkin' about the boy, too."

"The boy?"

"The boy should see the place. His daddy grew up down there, too."

The cousins followed them with their eyes, back and forth, back and forth.

"I suppose," said Mother. "But tonight? With the . . . funeral?"

"Just as well," said Joe. "Get his mind somewheres else."

"I see," said Mother.

"Might work for you too, Mae."

"Me?"

"Get your mind elsewheres."

She looked stunned, like a deer caught in the lamps of an automobile.

"Fine," she said. "We'll all go down together."

"It'll be good, Mae. You'll see."

Joe ate in silence then, and Mother continued to sit and stare at some mysterious spot on the table. The cousins ate little and quickly. As Joe filled his plate for a second time, Luke caught his mother's eye.

"May we be excused?"

Mother looked at him then at her niece. "You may," she said.

The cousins slipped away from the table.

"We'll be out in the yard," said Luke.

Mother nodded as they hurried out the door. They went around to the side yard. Rachel ran ahead to the tall poplar. Rings hung from one of its low, straight branches. She jumped up and grabbed the rings and began to swing. Gaining momentum, she whirled higher and higher, a blur of white and brown, arms springing like magical bands of energy. She slowed, then stopped and held herself perpendicular to the ground, legs together, shoes pointed, a perfect knife of white and brown. She swung down, hit the ground, and arched her back gracefully.

"My, my," said Luke.

Rachel blushed.

"Wanna try?"

"No way," said Luke.

"I can teach you."

"There's just no way I'm gonna learn."

Luke turned and walked back to the veranda. He sat on the steps and she joined him. They looked across the field. The sun had only moved slightly in the high, wide sky, but the light across the field had shifted, darkening the prairie grass.

"Do you think they're talking about it?" said Rachel.

"It?"

"About my mother, your father. The dying."

"I don't know."

"He talks about her all the time. And he talks like she's still alive."

Luke turned away, uncomfortable.

"He sits in his chair at home and looks to her place at the table and he goes on and on and on, like she was there in the room with him. He doesn't know that I hear him. And I don't even think he cares."

Mother banged open the screen door to the veranda.

"Does that dress need ironing for the morning?"

"It does, Aunt Mae. I can do it."

"I put the hot iron on the board in the back room."

Rachel touched Luke's arm. "Come watch me."

They went inside and down the hall into the back room. Mother had laid the dress out to be ironed. Rachel slipped behind the board and Luke sat up on the stool, opposite. There was a line of shirts behind her, a wall of stiff whiteness—his father's shirts, ironed before he left for Fort William.

"I don't have a suit," he said.

Rachel looked up from the ironing. "A suit?"

"For tomorrow. I only have pants, a shirt, and a sweater."

"That'll be fine."

"I just don't know. I should have a suit."

Rachel ironed in silence, pumping the steaming iron on the stiff black dress back and forth, her head down, sweating in the heat of the small room. The walls were peppered with lithographs cut from pages of the *Calgary Herald*, and sketches of the dresses Mother had hoped to make for the women moving into Cayley with the men being hired by the railway. Luke got up from the stool, circled the ironing board, and walked along the periphery of the room.

"This is mine now," he said.

"What?"

"This room. She said she wouldn't be sewing now that Daddy's gone. She'll be lookin' to work in town. And she wants me to have a bed and a desk and a lamp in here."

Mother opened the door. "Are you done with that?"

"I am," said Rachel.

"We'll be leaving now," said Mother.

They said nothing.

"We'll be out there in the automobile."

They stood in silence for a long moment, looking at the line of stiff white shirts. They heard their parents walking out the door. The cousins went into the kitchen and saw that the surfaces of the counter and the table were clean and shining. Then they went outside and climbed up into the back seat of the large black Maxwell.

Joe drove the automobile like his motorcycle, with fierce concentration and a taste for speed, holding the steering wheel like handlebars. Although the lane was rutted, they rattled down to the road, and once on the higher grade, he accelerated, driving up dust behind them in a great circular cloud. The road cut across prairie, only rolling occasionally as it rumbled alongside Highwood River, which rushed down from the mountains. After a while, they rolled up into the ranch lands, where the neat cut of sections gave way to the wilder freedom of undivided land. The river and the road leaned then to the north and again to the west, towards the chalky, jagged line of the mountains. They continued in silence, listening to the rumble of the motor, the sun still high on their left, arching slowly in its late summer trajectory.

They could smell the mountains before entering them, the cooler, sharper air fresh with the scent of pine and cedar; the road began to roll high and low, undulating as it climbed towards a mountain pass and the full rush of the river, its smell rich and running. The road followed a ridge above the river for a while then plunged down to the very floor of the valley. They passed old, broken homesteads with square-cut log houses and log barns overrun by the wild reach of the forest. The light began to fade and the shadows in the woods above the valley grew heavier and darker. Finally, they slowed down and turned into a lane overgrown with thick grass. The smell of the river was close and coming. A large two-storey wood building with a pitched roof and chimney reared up in front of them. A wide veranda with six hewn posts ringed the first floor, and the window holes on the second and third floors looked like empty eye sockets. They sat in the stillness and stared at the dark, heavy presence.

"I can't go in there," said Mother.

"It'll be fine," said Joe.

"I can't. I just can't."

"Well, we'll stay put and let the children go."

Joe climbed down from the driver's seat to let the cousins slip out. They walked across the field in front of the building, saw the stumps of heavy posts that once ringed the compound, and went up the steps of the building. Luke moved ahead and pushed open the front door. The fading sunlight swung into the dark hallway towards the back of the building, and there, through a window, they saw the rise of the newly full moon. They reached the window and looked across the stretch of high grass and saw the river, glittering like a silver and black bracelet.

"It's beautiful," Rachel said.

Luke stared at the running river and, in the silence, began to hear the building around him, the sounds of decay so close to this source of life. He felt her cool hand on his arm.

"What are you thinking?"

"Nothin'," he said.

"I'm thinking about her." She pointed towards the high grass. "She would play out there with your father in the summertime. And sometimes they would see the canoes coming down the river and sometimes the men in them would wave. She would help Grandma in the garden and he would help Grandpa with his horses and with the traders and it was all such a long time ago."

Luke turned and led her to the stairs, the building dark and heavy. When they reached the landing, he headed towards the back of the building to a small room, which looked down on the tall grass that led to the river. She came in and began circling the room.

"This was hers," she said.

"How do you know?"

"I just do."

She stood still then, in the centre of the room.

"She told me about the dances at the pavilion in High River. She would go with your father and she would wear a summer dress and they would dance and dance, and the moon must have been high and shining like it is tonight."

She began to dance around the room. The light through the window streaked the dark, stained walls.

"She would dance at home, too. She would put a roll on the piano and she would swing around the room with the music and her feet were as light as the wind and she would whirl me around and around."

"Like my Daddy and the rings."

"The dancing and swinging seem the same."

"They do," said Luke.

She came to him again, took him in her arms, and began to move him around the room, dancing, holding him, and the sweetness of her was there now, under the running smell of the river. And then she stopped.

"I almost think a lovely dress of hers could still be here."

She went to the closet in the corner and opened the door wide. The light danced wildly in the small, empty space.

"Oh, how I wish it were," she said.

She turned and went to the window, framed by the early evening light.

"She could never fit in back there in Saskatchewan. She said that the women came to see her in the beginning and told her things and brought her things, but then they stopped. When they found out Daddy was Métis. They just stopped. And then they whispered when she went to town and they whispered when she went to church and they whispered all the time. And she just didn't know why."

Rachel rushed from the room then. Luke followed her down the stairs through a back door. She stood on the steps leading down to the high grass under the brightening light of the moon and looked across the grass to the river. She turned to him.

"Do you know?"

"Know what?"
"About her."
"About who?"
"About my mother."
"What?"
"You can never tell a single soul."
"I won't."
"She didn't just die."
"She didn't?"
"Daddy lied to your father and your mother."
"Lied?"
"He said she was sick and she died."
"What happened?"
"She went to that high bridge over the wild river and she jumped and she drowned and they found her two days later and I never saw her again."

They stood on the steps in the stillness, looking at the black, moving river beyond the grass.

"He sat in the kitchen for days and days and talked to her chair like she was still alive. And sometimes he would call me by her name. And sometimes he would hold me like he used to hold her and it didn't feel right. And now I wish it had been him."

Luke took her in his arms and held her close and stroked her soft and shining hair. And then she pulled away from him. As he looked at the river, he suddenly felt a touch, like the dust of death, and shuddered. He waited for the shudder to pass, watching the run of the river, and, instead of seeing bright silver rivulets, saw only ropes of black, long and curling and alive.

"I don't know why she did it. I just don't know why."

The sound of her words was small and hollow and almost lost in the running of the river.

Joe came around the side of the house.

"There you are," he said.

Joe looked up at the round brightness of the moon. He draped his arms around them both, squeezing, digging his fingers into their arms.

"This is how I remember your father and mother."

Joe swung them around to face the river.

"A boy and a girl, the moon and the river."

They all shared a sudden shudder. Then Joe began to sob. The sob turned into a kind of low, long, ancient howl.

"And now they're gone."

A sound came to them from the distant woods, faint but resonant and answering, returning and echoing through the valley. And the howling was joined and became a chorus, and it seemed a tenderness of sound, echoing then dying deep within the woods. Wolves.

"They share the secret," said Rachel. "I just know they do."

2

In the morning the cousins slipped through the screen door into the yard. The day was dry and hot, and the dust at their feet was powdery and almost white. The black automobile stood on the white dust like a phantom from another place, another time. As they gathered around the Maxwell, Rachel brought her hand to her bare neck.

"I forgot something, Aunt Mae."

"Hurry on, honey."

Rachel turned and went back into the house to the small bedroom on the second floor. She picked up her mother's silver chain and cross from the chest of drawers. As she drew the chain over her head, she noticed the framed image of her mother and uncle as children. She shuddered and hurried from the room. The kitchen was spotless: the pine table and chairs, still damp, the counters scrubbed to a shine. Through the window, she saw her family in the yard gathered by the side of the big black Maxwell. She joined them.

"Did you find it?"

She touched the cold chain around her neck.

"I did, Aunt Mae."

Joe, behind the wheel now, leaned in and set the switch and then got out and went to the crank. He was wearing a black suit and one of his brother-in-law's stiff white shirts. His bony shoulders looked lost in the square shoulders of the suit. Rachel climbed into the back seat with her aunt, Luke into the front seat. Joe whirled the crank and the Maxwell sputtered to life. He got back in, turned the automobile into the lane, and headed towards the white spire of the church in Cayley, rustling dust behind them. Further to the west, the mountains were white with the light of morning, a chalky sketch on the horizon.

As they neared town, the gathering swell of people became clear. There were a few other automobiles and dozens of carriages filled with small groups of people dressed in black suits and dresses. There were mounted police as well, near the intersections of the small town, discretely placed at intervals, their sharp eyes scanning all vehicles heading towards the neat white church. The cousins noticed children watching from the flat roofs of buildings. They turned a corner and saw St. Rose Church and the black carriage with the pine coffin covered with wildflowers. Rachel ran her finger along the fine links of the chain around her neck. As they pulled in front of the church and entered the yard, six men in black coats came up from the basement. The man in the lead tipped his hat as he passed and, one by one, the other men tipped theirs, too.

They approached the coffin in the back of the carriage. Mother and the cousins got out of the Maxwell. Joe stayed behind the wheel. Mother circled around the car to the driver's door.

"I don't think I can do this, Mae."

"Do what?"

"Go in there."

"I…"

"It's like you last night."

"I see," said Mother.

"I just can't."

"As you wish, Joe."

"I'll drive by the garage and pick up some things for the cycle. I'll be back after . . . the viewing."

He engaged the clutch and pulled away. Mother went to the cousins.

"Uncle Joe's gone to get some things at the garage."

Rachel watched the car rush away, a knowing look on her face. Mother led them down the stairwell and into the basement. There was a dais at the back of the room with a rectangular wooden frame in the centre, flanked by two large candles. Neat rows of chairs faced the dais. Along the wall leading to the kitchen, there was a long table.

"I'd like you both to sit here a moment."

Mother was pale, without powder or rouge; the soft skin around her eyes was raw.

"Yes, ma'am."

Mother went down the aisle and, before reaching the dais, turned sharply into the kitchen. Women from the church were preparing trays of cookies and teacakes and pots of tea.

"Can I help?" asked Mother.

"There's no need, dear," said the woman in charge.

"I really need to."

"Ah," said the woman. "Why yes, of course."

"It's better to keep busy."

"Yes. To keep busy," said the woman.

Mother took her place alongside the women and, after a few moments, they continued the conversation they had been having when she first came into the room.

As Luke sat waiting and staring at the dais, the six pallbearers came down the stairs with the pine coffin on their shoulders. They made their way down the aisle to the dais then set the coffin on the wooden stand. One of the men lit the two candles. They retreated down the aisle again to assemble the crowd waiting outside.

Luke was drawn down the aisle and, on reaching the dais, stepped up and stood before the coffin. A lid covered the rough pine box, which was punctured with nail holes every twelve inches. The coffin seemed too small to him. He turned away and went to the back of the room and stood in the stairwell.

Mother came out of the kitchen, carrying a tray of cookies and teacakes. She set the tray on the table. Rachel quickly joined her and followed her into the kitchen. There were two kettles on the large, porcelain stove and on the table, more trays of cakes and cookies.

"I'll help with the tea, Rachel. Will you take one of these trays?"

Rachel ferried the tray to the table and, when she returned to the kitchen, went to her aunt's side. Mother was pouring water into one of the pots but suddenly stopped. A tremor struck her face and gave way to short, urgent sobs. She set the kettle down and took the girl into her arms.

The kitchen door opened. The funeral director came in and walked towards them. He froze for a moment, but then came ahead.

"Missus?"

Mother broke away from Rachel, smoothing the front of her dress. "What is it?"

The man pulled a watch from his waistcoat.

"It's time."

"I see," she said.

The man smiled nervously and backed out of the room.

"Please take one of the teapots. I'll bring the other."

Rachel picked up the brown pot and went into the other room. The funeral director was on the dais, lifting the lid from the coffin. She hurried to the table and set the pot down, her back to the dais. The basement door was open and, above the stairwell, men were talking. Luke was still hidden in the dim light of the stairwell, listening to the men.

"It was murder, pure and simple," said a man with an Irish accent.

"Damn you for sayin' that."

"I'm sayin' what's true, Eddie."

"Damn you."

"Listen, Eddie." The voice of another man. "He leaves the pickets and before he gets to the diner they stab him. Not one time, no. They stab him again and again."

"It was robbery."

"Robbery!" The first voice, broad and Irish. "He's got nothin' to rob. He's a railwayman. He's got no coin and surely no valuables."

"The police said it was robbery."

"The police is it? The police. They're the ones who likely did it, Eddie. Can't you see?"

"I can't see a thing."

"That's right, Eddie Steineman. You're old and blind and can't see a thing."

There was a sudden commotion, the sound of men stirring for a fight.

"Listen to me!" A new voice, young and high pitched. "There's a great fury in the men. They see it as murder and there's something needs to be done."

"And you listen to me," said Eddie, in a sure and decisive tone. "The boy was like a son to me. And now with his widow and his son here to mourn his passing, I want nothing but dignity. For them. For the memory of Timothy."

The words rushed over Luke like an avalanche. He turned and swept back into the room. Mother was with Rachel as he approached. She took her son's face in her hands. They were cold and dry.

"You must cry, Luke."

The flame of her tears in the kitchen had tinted her skin a copper shade.

"Will you?"

"I just can't. And I don't know why."

Mother held him tight and close again, bringing his face against her soft breast, stroking his hair. Luke inhaled the sweet, clean smell.

"Your father was such a good man, Luke."

Rachel looked at the cookies on the table. She took one in her fingers and felt the sprinkle of sugar. Luke came to her side and he, too, took one of the cookies.

Then there was a warm, large hand on his shoulder. He turned around and saw an old man with white hair and glasses, awkwardly wearing a new suit.

"Luke?"

"Yes, sir?"

"Do you remember me?"

Luke shook his head.

"I'm Eddie Steineman. I worked with your father."

The sugar on the cookie in his hand felt as sharp as salt.

"Your father was a good man."

The salt began to sting.

"And he's sure to be in Heaven."

Eddie took off his glasses and rubbed his eyes. He turned to Rachel.

"And you're Kate's girl?"

"I am."

"Where you staying?"

"With Aunt Mae and Luke. Me and my father."

"I was sorry to hear about your mother."

Rachel's hand went to the chain.

"Timothy and Kate were fine young people."

Luke and Rachel simultaneously looked away from the kind man in front of them and, instead, settled their gazes on the pine coffin on the dais.

Eddie turned to Mae.

"Missus Gallagher?"

"Yes?"

"I worked with Timothy. My name is Steineman. "

"He talked about you. The union . . ."

"If there is anything I can do . . ."

"Yes," said Mother. "Certainly."

Eddie turned away from them. The other five pallbearers returned to the basement. He joined them. Their suits hung on their bodies like they would hang in a closet—limp, without character. They hurried down the aisle and, reaching the dais, took positions behind the coffin. And as they settled behind the coffin, folding their hands awkwardly in front of them, men, women, and children began to flow into the room. Mae eased Luke and Rachel into chairs near the back of the room and, with them, watched the mourners.

They came with solemn urgency, as pilgrims might to a shrine. They coursed down the aisle, but on reaching the dais, each one became distinct for a moment, standing in front of the coffin. They moved then to the rows of chairs and held their heads still, looking towards the coffin, watching intently, without the usual flutter of movement or furtive whispering. The basement soon swelled with people. They were dressed modestly but with dignity: the women in long, dark dresses with shawls over their shoulders; the men in dark suits, stiff white shirts, and dark ties; the boys in short coats, knickers, stockings, shoes; and the girls, in shorter, severe dresses, dark stockings, and shiny shoes.

A tension began to build in the room. The pallbearers seemed to be a barometer of that tension. They stood absolutely still, but their eyes darted from the coffin to the widow and children in the back of the room. Father McCarthy slipped into the room from the kitchen and stopped by the door for a moment. He looked pale and nervous, not like himself at all. He wound his way through the mourners to Mae at the back of the room.

"I must speak to you, Mae," he said. He looked stunned, eyes wide but without focus.

"Please excuse us, children."

"Yes, Father."

Mother followed him to the stairwell. The soft summer air had drifted down into the basement.

"I've just left the bishop," he said. "He wants to cancel the procession to the cemetery tomorrow."

"But why?"

"He fears trouble."

"Trouble?" said Mother. "The trouble's already happened. This is the trouble. My husband was murdered and there's not a thing we can do about it."

"I said that."

"I believe there will be far more trouble if the people are denied their right to walk Timothy to his grave."

Mother turned away from him and went back into the room. She took Luke and Rachel by the hands then.

"It's time."

They walked slowly down the aisle, with dozens of eyes fixed on them. They stepped up on the dais and came as close to the coffin as they could. The pallbearers glared at the children. The eyes of five of the men had a steely urgency. Only Eddie's eyes were soft, compassionate.

Luke looked at the body in the coffin, waxen and cold, eerily without life. The face was set in serenity, with hands crossed, the nails perfectly clean. The suit was black and the shirt brilliantly white. And the silver band was still on his finger. Mae leaned into Luke.

"I'll leave you alone for a moment."

She stepped to the back of the dais.

Luke moved even closer. He knelt down and felt the rough pine floor through the thin cotton of his pants. He kept his eyes on the silver band on the finger. He felt as white as the shirt on the still body of his father.

"Goodbye, my da," he said.

There was a muffled crying behind him now.

"Goodbye."

Rachel joined him and knelt down, too. She took the silver chain and cross from her neck and held the cold silver in her hands. She looked at his frozen face. The lids of his once-fierce eyes were sublimely still. She gently set the chain and cross on his hands.

"From your sister, my mother."

The crying of the mourners rose, filling the space with anguish.

Mother was behind them now, her hands on their shoulders, drawing them away. She knelt in front of the coffin then, the children at her back. She clenched a handkerchief, but, like the children, did not cry. She simply looked at her dead husband, the father of their son, the brother of all the men in the room, the murdered man whose real story would never be known. She had steel in her eyes, cold and blue, like the mountain sky in the midst of winter. And the pallbearers behind the coffin were staring, too, with dead still eyes. The mood in the room shifted suddenly. There was an intense pause, similar to the short space of time before dynamite erupts. Mother stood then. She led the children from the dais and back down the aisle. The wailing stopped as she moved, and when they reached the chairs at the back of the room and sat down, the descending quiet crackled with imploding energy.

The funeral director went back to the dais. After the pallbearers helped him lift the lid back onto the coffin, he circled the rough pine box and pounded a dozen nails into the soft wood.

Then Father McCarthy came to the dais. He was no longer pale.

"My dear people," he said. "The mass will be at nine in the morning. And, following the mass, the funeral procession will move with Timothy to his resting place in the cemetery on Price's Hill."

Father McCarthy stepped down, and the pallbearers took their positions around the coffin. They squatted and lifted the coffin from the stand. Then they turned and, with the coffin on their shoulders, walked slowly down the aisle, through the room, up the stairs, and out into the bright sun.

And Rachel, leaning on her aunt, slipped her face into her aunt's lap and began to cry quietly and with great dignity. Luke looked at his mother and cousin with warmth in his eyes but a cold clarity in the set of his jaw. The room emptied quickly, and when they stood together moments later, they seemed to each find a source of composure to take them up the stairs and through the crowd and past the carriage with the coffin covered with flowers and into the waiting Maxwell and back to the farm. They all, even Joe, somehow moved through the rest of the day and into the evening with a kind of majestic peacefulness and went to bed while the light was still strong.

3

THE NEXT MORNING, EDDIE stood away from the other pallbearers in the shade of the portico behind one of the columns at the entrance of the church. The sky was a delicate blue, with soft tufts of clouds, and the early morning sun was shining on the growing mass of people on the street. The shape of the crowd spread organically as the mourners, dressed in shades of black and grey, continued to stream down the street. The only colours were the red armbands worn by the men and the blue uniforms of the police encircling the mass of people. Eddie moved closer to the other pallbearers, raising his hand to the red armband on his sleeve.

"It's not about murder," said a tall man. "It's about the men."

"Aye," said another.

"Timothy said the men must be organized."

Eddie came closer still.

"And how do we do this?" asked Eddie.

The tall man swung around. He looked at him as he would look at an old man trying to cross the cobbled street without assistance.

"What could you be meanin'?"

Eddie took a deep breath, expanding his already powerful chest, and drew his hands into whitening fists.

"You know what I mean."

"This has got nothing to do with you."

"Oh, it does."

"You're old, Eddie. This is for young men."

"It's for men. And I'm the one man they all know, now that Timothy is gone."

The crowd stirred suddenly.

Eddie stepped down from the portico and, in the rising sun, saw horses trotting with precision into the street. When the mounted division reached the crowd, they circled it and then took up positions on the periphery, between the policemen already there. The cortège turned into the street now. The carriage with the coffin was followed by another black carriage and, behind those, a snaking line of people. As the cortège neared the church, the crowd swelled, pushing against the line of horses and policemen. After some confused jostling, the line of blue receded.

The carriage with the coffin stopped. The pallbearers, easing the crowd away, took their positions on either side. The second carriage stopped. Mother and Joe, Luke and Rachel sat alertly, with their eyes ahead, oblivious to the swelling crowd around them. The funeral director climbed down from the carriage with the coffin and opened the tailgate. The pallbearers slid out the coffin and lifted it on their shoulders. They turned and waited. The crowd was silent, yet still surging, swaying towards the coffin. A tall man reached through the pallbearers and ran his large hand on the side of the coffin. The pallbearers held their ground, the coffin firmly on their shoulders, as others reached through and touched the rough pine. Mother and Joe climbed down from the second carriage and waited. Luke and Rachel joined them. Rachel seemed to shine with an aura of serenity. Luke maintained the stern set of his jaw. They took their places behind the coffin.

The pallbearers carried the coffin up the steps to the portico. The tall wooden doors were held for them. They walked into the baptistery and waited for the crowd to settle behind them. Then they moved into the narrow, high nave of the church, bathed in blue light from the stained glass windows. The organ sounded and the small, male choir chanted the first lines of "Dies Irae"; the sober, sad music soared to the high-arched ceiling. They reached the chancel gate and rested the coffin on the wooden stand. Then they turned and ushered the mourners into the pews. The church filled quickly; mourners lined the side and back aisles. Mother, Joe, Rachel, and Luke slipped into the pew at the very front of the church, near enough to the pine coffin to touch it.

As the sacristy bell sounded, Father McCarthy emerged holding a chalice and flanked by two altar boys. He was wearing a black chasuble with a purple cross embroidered on the front. He swung to the foot of the altar, genuflected, and carried the covered chalice to its place in front of the tabernacle in the centre of the altar. Then he returned to the foot of the altar to begin the Latin Mass of the Dead.

"*Introibo ad alatari Dei*," he said.

The altar boys responded. "*Ad Deum qui laetificat juventutem meam.*"

After he finished the prayers, Father McCarthy ascended the steps and undressed the chalice. He moved to the right side of the altar and, finding his place in the large, ornate missal, read the Epistle. The altar boy moved the missal to the other side of the altar. The priest followed and read the Gospel. There was a stirring among the mourners as he moved down the altar steps and advanced towards the pulpit. He mounted the spiral steps and stood before the sea of black in the pews. Then he reached under his vestments and took out a piece of paper. Before beginning, he searched for Mother's eyes.

The eulogy was spare and terse. He departed from the convention of seeking inspiration from the Mass of the Dead and instead began with a description of the life of St. Joseph, the simple life of any workingman. He moved quickly to the significance of such a life, inspired by the encyclical *Rerum Novarum* of Leo XIII, and paused after the important words: "justice," "solidarity," and "the rights of the workingman." After meeting the mourners' eyes, he turned to face Timothy in the coffin.

"He was a father and a workingman. And he was a man of great inner strength. The strength grew in him as he understood his mission." He stopped and swept his hand before him. "And you, dear brothers and sisters, were that sacred mission."

The mourners drew in their breath.

Father McCarthy returned to the altar and prepared for the Consecration. The altar boys brought the cruets to the side of the altar. Father McCarthy washed his fingers and cleaned the inside of the cold chalice, then poured in the wine. He returned to the centre of the altar and, bending over the chalice and the host, began to recite the words of Consecration.

He genuflected and raised the Host.

"*Hoc est corpus meum.*"

The altar boy sounded the bell.

Father McCarthy broke the Host and took the Eucharist then.

He genuflected again and raised the chalice.

"*Hic est enim Calix Sanguinis mei* . . ."

The altar boy sounded the bell again.

He genuflected and took the wine.

Father McCarthy moved quickly through the rest of the Mass, only pausing slightly at the end.

"*Ite, Missa est.*"

"*Deo gratias,*" replied the altar boys.

They returned to the sacristy and the mourners rose from their kneelers and sat back in their seats. A few minutes later, after the bell sounded again, an altar boy with a brass crucifix emerged from the sacristy, followed by two boys with candles, a boy with a censer, and one with a holy water font, and then Father McCarthy. As they moved to the communion railing, the congregation rose to its feet. The boys with the cross and candles continued to the foot of the coffin while Father McCarthy and the other two boys went to the head. He opened the thin missal and began to recite the prayers of blessing. The organ sounded then, and the deep, mournful chanting began again.

While the chanting continued, Father McCarthy circled the coffin with the censer, sending billows of incense rising into the nave. He circled the coffin again with holy water, shaking beads onto the surface of the lid. The beads sat for a moment then were absorbed into the wood. He closed the ceremony with the Sign of the Cross.

Father McCarthy moved around the coffin with the two altar boys. They joined the three other altar boys carrying the brass crucifix and candles. The pallbearers slipped from their pew and took the coffin on their shoulders again. Father McCarthy waited for Mother, Joe, Luke, and Rachel to fall in behind the coffin then started slowly down the aisle, moving with the mournful rhythm of *"Dies Irae."* The mourners fell in behind.

Illuminated by the blue light from the stained glass windows, the procession moved through the church, following the pace set by the music, and stopped at the front doors. They swung open, and sunlight angled into the baptistery and splashed on the surface of the coffin. The procession moved ahead then. The street was still filled with a round, milling mass of people encircled by horsemen and police. As the procession moved down the steps into the high sun and stopped, the waiting crowd began to ease behind the cross and coffin. The procession moved then, heading east, and filled the entire street. The horsemen and police moved from the curb to the sidewalk and took up positions on the procession's flanks. The mourners continued to stream from the church and join the moving mass of people, stretching two long blocks. By the time the church was empty, the procession involved hundreds of people.

The crowd was absolutely silent behind the brass crucifix, and the only sound was the steady scrape of feet over the cobblestones punctuated by the knocking of the horses' hooves on the sidewalk. Policemen on foot moved alongside the procession. They were no more than boys, for the most part, with eager, confused faces, likely the sons of the men and women in the procession. The horsemen were older, with the hard, professional looks of former soldiers, and the sergeants and officers walking alongside the young men were older, cynical men with faces corrupted by too much drink, too many compromises. Ahead, the police had pulled their wagons in formation to stop the procession from entering the block shared by city hall and the town jail. City hall was new, built with freshly quarried cream stone. It had a clock tower taller than any buildings in town. The jail on the south side of the street was low like city hall, fashioned from cream stone. The horsemen to the left trotted ahead and took up positions in the intersection, reinforcing the barricade behind them. The procession turned sharply at the corner and moved south, avoiding contact with both the horsemen and the men at the barricade. The mass of black and grey behind the brass crucifix marched with solemn assurance. A silent compact seemed to be holding. The compact insured there was no real need to protect city hall and the jail because the men, even the younger, militant men who had raised the spectre of violence the night before, had slipped into a kind of secret obedience to the order of the day, knowing not to risk what Timothy had, for fear that his fate would await them. That fate was just on the edge of town in the hole dug six feet into the fertile black soil. A murder would go unpunished, a riot averted, and orderly government would protect the disorder of a newly emerging capitalism in a new land.

4

Luke went outside before the rest had finished breakfast. He looked up at the sturdy, shining rings on the tree, remembering the day his father had brought them home from the rail yard—one of his occasional finds. He remembered watching his father shinny up the tree with thick rope from the barn and tie intricate knots to secure the rope to the branch. Later, standing on a stepladder, he had tied the rope to the rings in the same careful way. Then, in one of the magic moments where Luke was able to witness the true centre of his father's being, he watched him jump up and grasp the rings and wind around like a majestic athlete. Luke was tempted to try now, but before he could finally decide, Rachel joined him. She tapped his shoulder, almost alarming him.

"There you are," she said. "We missed you at the table."

Even as the surprise receded and he adjusted to her presence, he could not bring himself to speak.

"I wish we could talk."

Luke looked up to where the ropes were tied to the branch.

"Do you want to try now?" Rachel looked as though she desperately wanted to connect with him. But his silence seemed inevitable, tragic. "I could show you, Luke. It's not so hard."

The words moved him aside as if by magic.

Rachel stood between the rings and, in a quick, decisive movement, sprung from the ground, grasped the silver rings, and pulled herself up so that she was standing in the sky. Luke was stunned, as he had been when he first saw his father do the very same manoeuvre. And now Rachel began to rock gently, back and forth, and soon was twirling around as though her arms were living springs, and the sound mimicked the wind. She moved through a balletic routine then let go and soared back down to the ground.

"There!" she said.

They stood in silence for a moment.

"My father found these rings at the rail yard. He brought them home and tied them to the tree and would come out here and swing on them sometimes after supper. For some strange reason I never joined him. Maybe I was scared."

"I did something the same when I saw my mother dancing around the kitchen. I dreamed of being a ballerina. But she was so lost in her own dancing that I became . . . what? . . . too shy, too scared to ask her to teach me."

"And now they're gone."

"And now they're gone," she repeated.

Luke moved very close to her. They were both below the silver rings.

"Teach me," he said.

"Oh, Luke, I surely will."

And the cousins spent the morning in close connection, leaping to grab the silver rings. Luke began to move from fear to courage, Rachel from strength to confidence. They knew they did not have to talk about his father or her mother. They also knew the secret they shared. And now they were learning the hard lessons about who they were and where they were and what they were and, more than anything, what they might hope to be.

Acknowledgements

IN THIS PARTICULAR ITERATION of these stories being shared with the world, I would like to thank my daughters, who knew that as much as I loved the idea of pioneering e-publishing as a burgeoning medium, there's nothing quite like holding a book – particularly one that has one's own writing in it – in one's hand. Heather McLeod, in particular, was the push behind making this happen, but her sisters Krissa Fay and Kirstie McLeod were willing partners.

I'd also like to thank my wife, Fay Martin, for agreeing to step into the world of marketing hard cover books – even if she made me promise that the books awaiting distribution would be stored in my office, not hers. We both know that she is the one who will making the trips to the post office, or arrangements for copies to be dropped off hither and thither.

My thanks to Karen Sloan, white witch artist, who once more stepped up to create an image that captures the aura of this collection.

And as always, I'd like to thank Susan Toy for bringing this opportunity to my doorstep, and her wonderful team for making the process look easy and the finished product look good.

Photo credit: Angelica Blenich/Photographer

MICHAEL FAY STUDIED CREATIVE WRITING with W. O. Mitchell, Alice Munro, and Richard Ford through grants from Alberta Culture.

Twice-elected president of the Periodical Writers Association of Canada, he was also the founder of the Alexandra Writers' Centre Society in Calgary.

He has written five plays, including the award-winning *Never Such Innocence Again*. Michael lives in Minden, Ontario, with his wife, Dr. Fay Martin.

Made in the USA
Lexington, KY
09 September 2019